A GENTLE
CALLING

**Other Crossway books
by Donna Fletcher Crow**

Glastonbury: The Novel of Christian England

THE CAMBRIDGE CHRONICLES
Book Two—*Treasures of the Heart*

THE CAMBRIDGE CHRONICLES

BOOK ONE

A GENTLE CALLING

Donna Fletcher Crow

CROSSWAY BOOKS
WHEATON, ILLINOIS • NOTTINGHAM, ENGLAND

A Gentle Calling

Second edition published by Crossway Books
a division of Good News Publishers
1300 Crescent Street
Wheaton, Illinois 60187

Cover Design: Jack Foster

Cover illustration: David Yorke

First edition published in 1987 by Victor Books,
a division of SP Publications, Inc.

Second edition first printing 1994

First British edition 1994, ISBN 1-85684-110-3

Production and printing in the United States of America for
CROSSWAY BOOKS
Norton Street, Nottingham, England NG7 3HR

Printed in the United States of America

Library of Congress Cataloging-in-Publication Data
Crow, Donna Fletcher.
    A gentle calling / Donna Fletcher Crow.
      p.   cm.—(The Cambridge Chronicles; bk. 1))
     1. Methodists—England—History—18th century—Fiction.
2. Methodist Church—Clergy—Fiction. 3. Women—England—Fiction.
I. Title. II. Series: Crow, Donna Fletcher. Cambridge chronicles; bk. 1.
PS3553.R5872G53 1994 813'.54—dc20   93-9497
ISBN 0-89107-806-1

02		01		00		99		98		97		96		95		94
15	14	13	12	11	10	9	8	7	6	5	4	3	2	1

To Betty Waller
librarian, teacher, friend
who inspires all who cross her path
with a love of books.
I'm thankful our paths crossed.

The Cambridge Chronicles

"There are so few people now who want to have any intimate spiritual association with the eighteenth and nineteenth centuries . . .

"Who bothers at all now about the work and achievement of our grandfathers, and how much of what they knew have we already forgotten?"

—DIETRICH BONHOEFFER,
Letters and Papers from Prison

RIVER CAM

CAMBRIDGE
1870

MADINGLEY
ROAD

NORTH
HAMPTON
STREET

MAGDALENE BRIDGE

St. John's
College

SIDNEY STREET

Trinity
College

to Newmarket
Holy Trinity Church

PETTY
CURY

QUEEN'S ROAD

Senate
House

Back's of the college

ST. ANDREWS

Great
St.
Mary's
Church

Emmanuel
College

King's
College

BENET

Market
Place

WEST
ROAD

SILVER STREET

DOWNING STREET

Baptist
Chapel

REGENT STREET

Parker's
Piece

Fens

TRUMPINGTON STREET

Peterhouse

LENSFIELD ROAD

THE HILLS ROAD

Sheep's
Green

N

to
London

Newcastle

Miles 0   25   50   75
Kms 0 25 50 75

York

ENGLAND

Sandon Hall

King's Cliffe

Cambridge

Troy
House

Raglan

Badminton

Bristol

LONDON

Bath

Shoreham

Wells

Tunbridge
Wells

Canterbury

- - - - - - the circuit ride

LONDON

St. John's Wood

Regent's Park

EUSTON ROAD

EDGWARE ROAD

ALDERSGATE

The
Foundry

MOORGATE

MARYLEBONE

Tottenham
Court
Chapel

CATO

Mary-
lebone
Church

Piccadilly
Circus

Lincoln's
Inn

Paddington

OXFORD

PICCADILLY

FLEET

St. Paul's
Cathedral

Bayswater

PARK

St. James

BAYSWATER ROAD

Mayfair

Hyde
Park

KNIGHTSBRIDGE

PALL MALL

Kensington
Gardens

Grosvenor
Square

Ken-
sington

KENSINGTON

London
Bridge

South
Kensington

Buckingham
Palace

Surrey
Lane
Chapel

to
Osterley
Park

Brompton

ROAD

Westminster
Abbey

OLD BROMPTON

Chelsea

Parliament

Thames River

GROSVENOR ROAD

*N*ed, you're bleeding!" Catherine Perronet rushed across the room to her brother. "What happened?" She took his arm to lead him to a chair, but he drew back sharply.

"Don't touch it, Cath. It may be broken."

"Broken!" This was too much even for Catherine's usually unruffled calm. "Were you attacked by a mob again?"

Edward Perronet smiled weakly. "I attempted to sow the seeds of truth to a crowd at Brixton. Shall we just say they were stony soil?"

"Apparently they found plenty of stones to hurl at you." Catherine started after a bowl of water and some rags. "We must call a doctor for your arm, but I'll wash your wounds first. If Durial sees you like this, I wouldn't vouch for the safety of your future child."

"Pray, do clean me up, Sister, though I would guess that Durial will be more distressed for her chair cover and carpet than for our child." He looked at his boots caked with fresh mud from the April rains.

Catherine directed a servant girl to bring a roll of bandages and sent the stable boy into Greenwich for the doctor. When she had staunched the flow of blood from her brother's head wounds and had cleansed all the caked blood and mud from his hair and face, she paused. "I must say, Ned, this is a fine way to make your homecoming after three weeks' absence. I suppose the family of an itinerant preacher should become accustomed to such behavior, but still you could have sent us some word of your progress in Wales. Were you beaten there too?"

Ned raised his tall, lanky body straighter in the chair, moving carefully to protect his damaged arm. His expression became suddenly serious, far graver than it had been over his physical injuries. "Sit down, Catherine. I have news I didn't want to put in a message. I fear it may distress you."

Catherine sat with quiet dignity. "In that case, let us have it quickly."

"My stay in Wales was extended because I attended the marriage of Charles Wesley to Miss Sally Gwynne."

Catherine stared at her brother. She heard the words, but her mind refused to make sense out of them. "Charles is married? Charles Wesley?" *My Charles?* "But I thought . . . I hoped . . . I was almost sure . . ." She forced a little hiccup to cover what wanted to come out as a sob.

"Forgive me, Ned. I fear I have been indulging in foolish fantasies. But after you told me I was on the list of women John Wesley thought would make eligible wives for his brother—"

"That was most unwise of me. I should never have told you."

"On the contrary, the information provided me many happy fancies with which to while away dull hours. You made it quite clear that there were three names on the list and that Sally Gwynne's was among them. I fear that I simply relied too much on the fact that Catherine Perronet was first on the list."

"And lest you hear from another and think me a traitor, I must also tell you that the letter I carried to Mrs. Gwynne from our father was instrumental in winning that reluctant lady's approval to the match."

"You and Father both? And what of our own Charl? Surely you knew he had spoken of a fondness for Miss Gwynne too."

Ned nodded. "Yes, I am fully aware that many hopes will be disappointed."

"If you carried a letter to Mrs. Gwynne, you must have known what was to take place. Why didn't you tell me?"

"I had an idea it was likely. I knew Charles hoped most fervently. But I also knew her parents had not consented and might not, so I wished to spare you pain in case nothing came of the matter."

He rose and crossed the room to take his sister's hand. "I'm sorry to be the bearer of news that wounds you so deeply, Catherine. But I thought it best to come from one who loves you. I wish I could say something to ease your pain."

She shook her lace-capped head of rich, dark curls and forced a trembly smile. "It's nice to know someone loves me, Ned." She withdrew her hand and resumed her composed posture. "Now I think you had best finish what you've begun and tell me about the lady . . . at least that she is worthy of so great a prize."

"I can assure you that Sally Gwynne is a fine musician and a beautiful young woman. And she is from one of the first families in that part of Wales."

"Fah, that is not what I wish to hear. Will she make . . . the Reverend Mr. Wesley a good wife? Will she keep him comfortable? Support his work? Make him happy?"

"Yes. As far as it's possible to predict such things, I believe she will do all that. She's much younger than he, by twenty years I should think, but she has the heart of one much more mature. When Mrs. Gwynne tried to make Charles promise never to return to Ireland where he was nearly stoned last month, Sally jumped to her feet and said, "'Indeed, I shall go with him!'" Ned paused before driving the final nail. "And Charles is much in love with her."

Catherine nodded, then turned slightly away so that her brother could not see the tears that brimmed in her eyes no matter how staunchly she ordered them not to. "Thank you, Ned. I am content. At least, I shall be soon." She stood, shook out the panniers under her wide blue skirt, and checked to see that the fine lawn fichu at her neck was in place. "I believe I hear the wheels of the doctor's carriage on the gravel. I shall prepare my sister-in-law for the shock of receiving her battered husband. But don't forget to put on a clean jacket before you present yourself to her."

Durial Perronet was resting in her room upstairs, her curtains drawn against the midmorning sun and a cloth of lavender water folded on her brow. It was indeed fortunate that the Perronets received a good income from their family estates in France, for no mere itinerant Methodist preacher could afford to keep such a wife as Durial.

"Am I disturbing you, Sister?" Catherine asked.

Durial sat up, carefully laid the lavender-water cloth on the marble stand by her bed, and arranged the neckline of her sprigged cotton dressing gown. "I am happy for a visitor. What is all the coming and going I hear below?"

"Ned is returned from Wales."

Durial pulled back her sheets without care for wrinkling them. "My husband home and I not told? Oh, where are my slippers?"

Catherine produced the slippers from under the four-poster bed.

"He will join you in a few minutes. But I must tell you first—there was an altercation—"

"Oh, no." Durial sank back on her pillows. "Was he stoned again?"

"I'm afraid so. But he was not injured badly—except for his arm. The doctor is with him now."

"Doctor! Oh, why won't he give up this dangerous enthusiasm and take a settled parish? I don't ask him to stop preaching, although I could wish he gave more time to his hymn-writing; but why can't he be a respectable vicar like his father? Your father has been settled at Shoreham for thirty years, and your mother didn't have to bear any of her twelve children while in fear for her husband's life."

Catherine was still doing her best to reassure Durial when Ned entered, his arm in a sling. "Edward," Durial said, "if I weren't so glad to see you, I should give you the thorough scolding you deserve. If you don't take any thought for your wife's nerves, at least you might think of your son." She put her hand to her waist where evidence of new life was just beginning to show.

"If you will excuse me, I shall leave you two to sort this out. I must get to work. The children should find their teacher in her place." Catherine crossed to the door.

"Cath, you aren't going to the Foundery today? Not after— everything?" Ned turned away from Durial. "I'll send a message that I am unable to drive you. The wrist is not broken, but still—"

"Fah! Our father taught me to drive when I was twelve years old. One of the stable boys can accompany me." Ned started to protest, but she stopped him. "Please. I would much rather be alone."

She tied a broad-brimmed hat of leghorn straw firmly under her chin, drew a bottle-green wool cape around her shoulders, and proceeded to the stables.

Catherine had never been more thankful for her work with the Methodist Society or of the long drive from Greenwich to Moorfields. She needed solitude. Catherine had always felt deeply, but in spite of her intense feelings, or perhaps because of them, she needed to examine the true state of her mind. She did not want sympathy or company; she wanted uninterrupted time. Whatever was to come to her, she could find the strength in God to face it; but she must understand her feelings first.

"You will sit up in back, Joseph, and be very quiet."

"Yes, Miss." The lad scrambled up on the box, and those were the only two words Catherine heard from him.

Old Biggin knew the way to the Foundery as well as Catherine, so she could give her full mind to Ned's devastating news. The fact that her dear Charles would be happy was a consoling thought; but all her dreams of being the one to make him happy, of sharing his work in close companionship, of singing his hymns with him . . . Well, she would simply have to amend her dreams. After all, it wasn't as if Charles had ever offered any concrete encouragement for such fancies. But the dreams had been so real to her.

No, they had been more than dreams—or at least she had believed them to be. Certain this was God's will for her life, she had often claimed Psalm 32:8: "I will instruct thee and teach thee in the way which thou shalt go: I will guide thee with mine eye." But how could she believe the Lord was guiding her when a beautiful young girl from Wales could shatter everything?

Catherine picked up a book from the bag at her feet—*Pilgrim's Progress*. It was her favorite, next to the Bible. She held the reins in one hand and left Biggin to plod down the country lane toward the Thames. With less than half an eye on the road, Catherine let the book fall open to its most-read passage:

> . . . just as Christian came up with the Cross, his burden loosed from off his shoulders, and fell from off his back, and began to tumble, and so continued to do, till it came to the mouth of the Sepulchre, where it fell in . . .
>
> Then was Christian glad and lightsome, and said, with a merry heart, "He hath given me rest by His sorrows, and life by His death." Then he stood still awhile to look and wonder, for it was very surprising to him that the sight of the Cross should thus ease him of his burden. He looked, therefore, and looked again, even till the springs that were in his head sent the waters down his cheeks . . .

She laid the book down. Today that joyful scene brought cold comfort, for it reminded her of her own conversion; and although the joy and exultation of that moment were still alive in her soul, her heart couldn't disconnect the spiritual experience from the earthly. Her mind mocked her heart with the fact that it had been Charles Wesley's preaching that had brought her to that sublime experience—doubly sublime because she had met her Savior and Charles at the same time.

Of course, no child of the godly Vincent Perronet could be far from a knowledge of God or a desire to do right. Catherine, always grave and thoughtful, had from her earliest days tried to keep the commandments and to please God and man. But the trouble was, she had never been *sure*, never completely satisfied that she had done enough to please God. Her parents and numerous brothers and sisters were quick to tell her in no uncertain terms if she failed to please them: "Cath, you forgot to lock the gate, and the cow could have gotten out." "Catherine, you tore your skirt again." "Your sums are all wrong." Not that these things happened often or that her family was hard on her, but her sensitive nature took each reproach far more seriously than the childish offense deserved.

But God was not so direct. How could she be *sure* she would someday hear, "Well done, My child; enter into My rest"? And so for twenty-one years Catherine had prayed and read her Bible and toiled to do good to those around her, hoping to find salvation—until that glorious summer day when Ned took her to hear Charles Wesley preach in the fields near Oxford. Charles had prayed with Edward when he had received the faith a few days earlier, and Ned was anxious for his sister to find the same assurance.

Catherine could still see the daisies bending on their slender stems in the long grass, feel the gentle sun on her head, and smell the freshness of God's earth whenever she thought of that meeting. They had sung Charles Wesley's hymn: "Jesus, Thine all-victorious love / Shed in my heart abroad; / Then shall my feet no longer rove, / Rooted and fixed in God." Catherine was certain she had heard an angel sing along with Charles's sweet voice as he led the singing.

And the words of his sermon had brought joy to her soul. Now she *knew* she was God's child. The warmth of the sun on her head and the warmth of the Son in her heart had fused in an ecstatic moment of light to drive all darkness of doubt from her mind and soul. From that moment she had never doubted God or her acceptance by Him. And from that moment also, she had never doubted her love for Charles Wesley.

Now her attention came back to her driving as she guided the gentle horse across London Bridge, lined with shops and bustling with traffic. Back in a more quiet street, she returned to her reminiscing. There had been three wonderful years of growth in her assured relationship with God and in her friendship with Charles—working with him and the others of the Methodist band at the Foundery, attending his meetings when he was preaching in London or when she could get Ned to take her to a nearby area, singing with him when he visited in their home.

Since her conversion, she had made her home with Ned and his wife so she could work regularly with the Methodist Society. And last year she began teaching in the day school with twelve students in her charge. She had not made the move just to be closer to Charles. Her supreme reason had been to express more fully her joy and her thanksgiving to God for His perfect salvation and for loving her; she wished to "labor more usefully in the vineyard," as so many Society members were fond of saying. She wanted to fulfill the purpose God had for her life. For with the assurance of her salvation came also the assurance of His guidance, and she had never wavered in this assurance . . . until now.

How could she be sure of God's leading when something so important—so fundamental to the foundation of her life—could go so devastatingly wrong?

But she still had her Savior. God was in His heaven, and He was here to share her day—all her days. And she had work to do. She clucked to Old Biggin, urging him to a faster pace along City Road. Soon she pulled up before the large white building that had been an abandoned foundery in ruinous condition before John Wesley purchased and reconditioned it. Now the galleried chapel could hold seventeen hundred people, with a smaller chapel to the back, a day school, private apartments, and rooms for many other Society activities.

Catherine left the carriage to Joseph's care, crossed the cobbled courtyard, and entered the deserted schoolroom, making sure each bench was straight and the floor spotless. The Foundery school educated sixty poor children under Headmaster Silas Told and two other masters, with the help of two female teachers. The children began their day at five o'clock by listening to preaching and then attended classes from six until twelve. After a midday meal, they returned to their studies from one until five in the afternoon. Catherine instructed the younger students in reading, and Miss Owen supervised the girls' needlework, which was sold to benefit the school. A frilled shirt brought two shillings, a plain shirt one shilling. The remaining instruction, primarily of writing, casting accounts, and studying Holy Scripture, was in the hands of the masters.

"Good morning, Miss Perronet." Her first pupil had arrived. Red-headed Isaiah Smithson took his seat on the front form. The others filed in behind him.

Teaching reading was usually Catherine's greatest joy—opening young minds to the wonder of language, giving them the ability to read God's Word. Of the sixty children attending the Foundery school, fewer than ten paid their own tuition; the others were so poor that they were taught, and even clothed, gratuitously. Catherine looked at the small heads bent over their books. What chance would any of them have to know the Savior or have a better life if it weren't for the Society? But today the job seemed unendingly tedious.

After a review from their abecedarian, Catherine asked her pupils to take out their primers. "Isaiah, will you please read the first lesson aloud."

Isaiah stood and rubbed his freckled nose with the back of a grubby hand. "Christ is the t-t-tr . . ."

"Truth," Catherine supplied.

"Truth. Christ is the l-l-light. Christ is the way. Christ is my life. Christ is my—" He came to a complete stop.

"Savior." Catherine suppressed a sigh of impatience.

"Christ is my hope of gl-gl-glory," Isaiah finished. Catherine reminded herself of John Wesley's admonition to his teachers: "We must instill true religion into the minds of children as early as possible. Laying line upon line, precept upon precept, as soon as they are able to bear it.

"Scripture, reason, and experience jointly testify that inasmuch as the corruption of nature is earlier than our instructions can be, we should take all pains and care to counteract this corruption as early as possible. The bias of nature is set the wrong way; education is designed to set it right."

Catherine looked at Isaiah's bruised jaw and scabbed knuckles, undoubtedly won from scrapping with ruffians in the street. She breathed a prayer of thanks that he and his brother and sisters were all in the school, no matter how tedious it was to listen to his halting reading.

She moved on to the lesson in moral precepts. The students read silently and then responded to the printed dialogue following the brief table. "What is the usefulest thing in the world?" she asked.

"Wisdom," they responded.

"What is the pleasantest thing in the world?"

"Wisdom."

At last when Catherine pulled out the watch tucked in her waistband, she saw it was time to release her students for the midday meal and prayers. Each child placed an abecedarian and primer on the table and filed from the room in orderly fashion. Clearly, the school had succeeded in instilling that meekness which John Wesley prescribed for young minds.

All except Isaiah Smithson. He shuffled his feet at the end of the line, hands behind him, eyes on the floor. "You shall miss your bread and pease porridge if you don't hurry along, Isaiah." Catherine tried not to sound impatient.

"Yes 'um, Miss Perronet. I jest wanted to say good-bye."

"Well, good-bye, Isaiah. I shall see you tomorrow."

"No, Miss. That's not what I mean. I'll not be comin' back."

"Isaiah, what are you talking about?" She saw a tear glisten at the corner of his eye.

"Me da' lost his job at the docks. Me and Esther and Samuel got to sweep."

Catherine's mind drew a sordid picture of what those few words meant. The two older children would spend their days and most of their nights sweeping horse droppings from the dusty street crossings in hopes that fine ladies who wanted to cross without soiling their skirts would reward them with a farthing. Isaiah was smaller, too small to defend his place at a crossing against bigger boys and small enough to be sent up a chimney to sweep. Altogether the children might earn a penny or two a day to supplement what their mother could make taking in washing. Catherine could only hope that the little bit wouldn't be spent on gin by an idle father.

"Isaiah, we shall see what can be done about this. Perhaps the Methodist Lending Society—I shall look into it."

Isaiah's blank look told Catherine he had no idea what she was talking about.

"Well, I shall tell you good-bye for the moment only. Isaiah, if I give you a primer, will you promise to take very good care of it and have Esther help you read in it every night?"

"Oh, yes, Miss. I will."

Catherine wished she could feel as sure as he sounded, but she must do something to keep the flicker of knowledge burning in this young mind. She placed the small brown book in his hands. "Isaiah, if you persist in your reading, you will find all that's necessary in here—the Creed, the Lord's Prayer, the Ten Commandments, even a chapter on manners."

"Miss Perronet . . ."

"Yes?"

"You sure are pretty." And he ran out the door, leaving the echo of a sniff behind.

In the empty room Catherine suppressed a desire to cry out, "Why, God?" Instead she straightened the already tidy tables before crossing the courtyard to the small chapel at the back of the Foundery. Even at midday the room with its small windows and dark wood was cool and dim. She knelt at the altar and thought again of Charles, of Isaiah . . . She groped her way through her own darkness.

Her one solace was her teaching, and now she was to lose her favorite pupil. She had been so happy to feel she was helping bring about the will of God for Isaiah and his family. But now that was to be taken away from her too.

If God was leading at all, was He leading in another direction? Maybe she was to leave the Foundery. Maybe she should not make her home with Ned and Durial. Nothing seemed to be working right for anyone in her life. Maybe, maybe . . . She didn't know, couldn't even guess. She felt as if she had nothing to care about. Her hands on the altar clenched with tension as she sought something to hold to.

She must care about something, if not Charles, if not her teaching, at least something, someone. And as soon as her mind formed the question, her heart answered, "God." She must care about Him, believe that He cared about her. That was the still, fixed point in her universe. If God dissolved into the maybe, she would be truly lost.

Perhaps she had misunderstood what she thought was God's way for her. But wouldn't the Shepherd be capable of making the sheep understand? Maybe . . . maybe . . . Her thoughts slowed, groping for the idea. . . . Maybe this was all part of the process. Maybe the Shepherd was lovingly leading her through a dark valley where she couldn't see the path. . . .

As she unclenched her fingers and relaxed, she became aware that she was not alone in the chapel. A tall, gaunt form was kneeling at the far end of the altar. His black suit and hose told her he must be a preacher; his pale blond hair was not powdered, but tied back neatly with a black ribbon. It was Philip Ferrar whom Ned had introduced to her just before his trip to Wales.

Catherine supposed she should leave Philip to pray in solitude, but she was caught by the earnestness of his posture and face. Ned had told her that he had held a curacy somewhere in Sussex and was now seeking another living. Strange. Ned hadn't explained why he left his position and was now doing itinerant preaching. The normal thing would have been to stay in Sussex until he found something else. She couldn't help thinking that the position he left couldn't have paid very well—he didn't look as if he'd ever eaten a really full meal. Even in the dimness, Catherine could see the patch on the elbow of his coat and the holes in his shoes.

As if suddenly aware of her observation, he ended his prayer and looked her way before she had time to bow her head discreetly. They regarded one another for a moment, and then both walked silently from the chapel. In the courtyard he paused. "Miss Perronet, may I hope you recall our introduction some weeks ago? I must ask you to forgive my intrusion on your prayers."

"Indeed, I remember, Mr. Ferrar. But I'm afraid it was I who intruded on you."

"No." He put on the tricorn hat he carried under his arm. "I had nothing more to say."

The forlornness of the words struck her because that was just how she felt. She looked at the hollows under his deep blue eyes. "Mr. Ferrar, my brother has just returned from Wales, and I believe you were about to make a journey to Hereford when we met. Won't you come to dinner tomorrow night? I am sure you and Ned will have much to talk about."

He accepted her invitation with a formal bow and with such seriousness that she abandoned her usual reserve. "Mr. Ferrar, you appear troubled. Mr. Wesley admonishes us to bear one another's burdens. Do you wish to speak of anything? I should be happy to pray for you."

Again he bowed slightly. "I appreciate your care, Miss Perronet. But the problem is not a new one. I went into Hereford in hopes of securing a living I had been told was open, but was turned down without an interview because of my Methodist enthusiasm. I shall, of course, continue my itinerant preaching if that is the way God chooses, but I do yearn to shepherd a settled flock." He paused. Her silence encouraged him to continue.

"It is always the same. There were many converts after my meetings in Hereford, but then I was forced to leave them. Lambs who had just set their feet on the path I had to abandon to all the wolves the devil can send. God knows my desire is to stay among them, nurture them, watch them grow. But it seems that it is not to be.

"Forgive me, Miss Perronet, I did not mean to weary you with my troubles. It was most kind of you to concern yourself with me."

"I assure you, I am not at all wearied, sir." Indeed, she felt she would like to know more of this strange, stiff man with the kind, troubled eyes. "My brother will be happy to receive you tomorrow evening."

Philip watched Catherine cross the courtyard to the stables, her wide blue skirts just brushing the cobbles. He turned and walked slowly through Bunhill Fields toward his furnished room upstairs in Mrs. Watson's rooming house. He climbed the dark stairs to his room. The "furnished" part of the arrangement was an iron bed with sadly sagging springs guaranteed to produce a backache, a washstand with a cracked bowl and miniscule blackened mirror, a creaking straight chair, and a chest. There was a window for fresh air if one could pry it open and a fireplace for warmth if one could endure the smoke.

In the months he had lived in the room, Philip had done nothing to relieve the starkness, perhaps because it was comforting in its likeness to the orphan asylum he had grown up in.

Yet, compared to the orphanage, Mrs. Watson's boarding house bespoke opulence. A small shelf of books was his only effort to make the room his own. Other than those few volumes, the space between the four whitewashed walls was as cold and impersonal as if Mrs. Watson still had the To Let sign in the window.

Only once in his thirty years had he really taken possession of a place by putting something of himself in it, and that had brought disaster. He had put everything he had, heart and soul, into his curacy in Midhurst, his enthusiasm carrying over even into furnishing his cottage. He had polished a Jacobean table he found in the attic under the thatched roof and then had so praised the pot of flowers the housekeeper set on it that she prided herself in always keeping it full, if only of holly sprigs in the winter. She saw that the rag rug on the hearth was shaken every day. And she kept the teacup on the little drop-leaf table freshly washed for the young curate to use when he sat by the fire at night to complete his day's reading.

That so much contentment and peace should have ended in such bitterness and hurt left a scar that Philip no longer expected to heal. But at least he had learned to live without leaving anything of himself about—without putting down any roots that could suffer such an emotional amputation. As he had just been refused for yet another vacancy, it appeared he might never be faced with the temptation to put down roots.

If the longing in his heart for a settled parish was from God, as he believed it to be, was he wrong to cling to the Methodist tenets that barred him from such a life? But what would be the good of having a congregation if he couldn't really share the gospel with them and lead them in the way of salvation to knowledge of a personal God? No, as long as he had breath in him, he must proclaim God's truth as he knew it. And that meant another preaching tour next week. With such a schedule there was no danger of his putting down roots even if he tried.

*A*fter an unusually violent bout of morning sickness, Durial was more than happy to leave the ordering of dinner for her husband's guest in the hands of her sister-in-law. So the next day Catherine could fulfill her wish of setting a really full meal before the painfully thin Mr. Ferrar.

But Durial joined the party to do her duty as hostess and serve from the top of the table. The Perronet household had readily taken to the new "French ease" method of table service whereby the master and mistress carved and served the dishes before them at each end of the polished mahogany table, before the guests helped themselves to the other dishes. "May I cut you another slice of beef roast, Mr. Ferrar?" the hostess asked.

Philip declined the sirloin, but accepted another serving of oyster loaf, and Edward served Catherine a slice of boiled turkey with prune sauce. "You are doing very well with your injured wrist, Ned."

"Yes, thank God it wasn't broken. What a nuisance that would have been. Afraid it will take awhile for some of these bruises to heal though." Ned gingerly touched a swollen spot on his forehead.

"Pray, don't let's talk of such unpleasant things." Durial

averted her eyes from her husband's wounds. "Tell us of the more pleasant aspects of your trip, Ned. What of the wedding?"

Edward hesitated, not wanting to distress his sister. "Yes, Ned. Tell us." Catherine's voice was composed.

"Charles had kept it so quiet we were all rather surprised to learn that he had been courting Miss Gwynne almost since he first met her four years ago when he was holding service with Howell Harris near her home in Garth. She attended that day with her father, Marmaduke Gwynne, who, as magistrate of the county, came with a warrant in his pocket to arrest the irregular preacher. But Gwynne was a fair man and wouldn't arrest a man without hearing him preach first. As it turned out, he was converted."

"And his daughter?" The lace lappets of Catherine's ruffled cap fell across her shoulders as she leaned forward.

"Oh, the whole family was soon converted and, it seems, all quite smitten with the younger Wesley brother. All except Mrs. Gwynne, who holds the accounts in the family and had some-one of a higher station in mind for her eldest daughter."

Durial swallowed a delicate bite of fish. "La, is that why it took Mr. Wesley four years to bring it about?"

"There were many hindrances, his lack of a settled home, her age—she's twenty years younger, you know—the fear of causing trouble in the Society."

"Trouble?" Durial asked. The conversation had now become a dialogue between the host and hostess with Catherine and Philip giving their full attention to the stewed venison.

"Yes, John especially feared that the many disappointed hopefuls for both Sally's and Charles's affection might cause dis-sension in the Society." Edward showed his discomfort at stating that in front of his sister and rushed on. "But Charles provided an acceptable marriage settlement from his book sales, and our father's letter seemed to soothe away some last-minute problems."

"How enchanting to hear such a charming story, my love."

Durial smiled across the candle-lit table. "And now everyone is blissfully happy."

Edward gave his wife an uneasy smile and turned to his plate.

Catherine, relieved that the painful talk seemed to be dropped, looked at their guest across the table and realized that he had spoken hardly a word during the entire first course. Indeed, instead of the good effect she expected her excellent meal to produce, he seemed more tense and drawn than before. This made his nose seem even larger and his dark blue eyes darker yet in startling contrast to his pale hair. She would have dearly loved to say something to put him at ease, but her own reserved nature could find no light words. At Durial's direction, the servant removed the first course and replaced it with another pattern of dishes bearing anchovy toasts, potato pudding, strawberry fritters, and jam tarts.

Edward turned to their guest. "And what of your work, Ferrar? Is the life of an itinerant suiting you?"

"If it suits our Master, I shan't complain."

Ned smiled and shook his head. "You're a man of few words. I should like to hear you preach. I think you might easily avoid the trap of tediousness, as John Wesley admonishes us."

"Would you truly, Edward?" Philip raised his fine, dark eyebrows in question. "I should be most happy of your companionship on my next tour. Someone to lead the singing would be more than useful, as my abilities in that area are woeful."

Ned opened his mouth to reply, but Durial spoke first. "Indeed not, sir. My husband is not yet recovered from the treatment he received at the hands of the last mob he sought to evangelize. If the rabble insists on going to the devil, I cannot see why you shouldn't leave them to it."

"My treatment was nothing compared to that received by our Lord and His disciples, and that was not His attitude, my love." Edward's reproof to his wife was gently delivered.

"You are right, of course. Forgive my temperamental state."

Her apology included Philip as well. "But I must ask you not to tempt my husband into danger before his wounds are healed."

"I would do nothing to distress you, Madam, but there should be very little danger in Canterbury. I have received many letters from Society members throughout Kent requesting a preacher."

"But, Ned . . . ," Durial began and then laid aside her fork with a sigh. "I know I waste my breath. You must excuse me if I withdraw now. I find I cannot keep late hours."

"I shall come with you, Sister." Catherine began to rise.

"No, Cath, please don't trouble yourself on my account. Audrey will help me. You stay and serve our guest."

Catherine settled back. She served pink pancakes to Philip and her brother as the men continued to discuss Philip's upcoming preaching trip. "My father has a farm at Canterbury I should be happy to see to. And from Tunbridge Wells we could come up through Shoreham," Ned said. "I should much like to visit our parents."

"But what of your injuries and—the other objections? I fear I shouldn't have spoken so rashly."

Ned smiled. "My wife is overly careful for my safety. She will get on much better without me here to mess up the house with my books and sheets of music."

Her serving finished, Catherine felt it was time for her to withdraw, but again her attempt to exit was thwarted. "Don't leave us, Cath. If I'm to serve as musician to Mr. Ferrar's evangelistic efforts, I should give him a demonstration of what he's in for. Let's have a bit of music."

That was a request Catherine always granted with eagerness, although she hoped Ned would not choose to sing one of Charles Wesley's hymns. She led the way into the parlor and seated herself at the harpsichord while Ned lit the tapers with a stick from the fireplace. The candlelight shimmered on the holly leaf pattern of her blue damask skirt; the three tiers of Valenciennes ruffles fell gracefully from her elbows as she fingered the keys. The lace was the finest French bobbin work, and Catherine spared a thought for her aunt in France who kept her well supplied in fashionable finery.

"What shall I play, Ned?" She ran a scale up and down the keys, the bright silvery tones of the harpsichord responding to her quick touch.

"Here." He set a piece of music before her. "Let's begin with this by our friend Count Zinzendorf. 'Jesus, Thy blood and right-eousness . . .'" His rich tenor filled the room. "'Thou hast for all a ransom paid, for all a full atonement made.'"

"Come, come, Philip. You must join us." Edward placed another sheet of music on the rack. "You sing too, Cath. This old Welsh hymn melody is best with a group of voices."

Catherine hesitated at the words her brother had put before her. Was it a random selection, or did he guess at her spiritual struggles? She forced her fingers to play and hoped her light soprano voice could stay on tune without wavering. "Guide me, O Thou great Jehovah, / Pilgrim through this barren land; / I am weak, but Thou art mighty, / Hold me with Thy powerful hand. . . ."

The words sank into her heart as vocalizing the prayer brought its own pledge of faith. Her voice grew stronger on the second verse. ". . . Let the fiery, cloudy pillar / Lead me all my journey through; / Strong Deliverer, be Thou still my strength and shield. . . ."

She had been caught up in the song as the Lord assured her through its words that He would lead her. It wasn't until the repeated refrain that her ear caught the discordant note behind her. The voice didn't lack strength, just correctness of pitch.

She was caught off guard and gave a gurgle of laughter before she realized what she had done. The dissonance stopped at once. She turned to their guest, afraid she had wounded him by her thoughtlessness.

But instead of seeing pain on his countenance, she met the merriest twinkle she had seen in his blue eyes and a smile so broad it balanced the size of his nose. It was the first open emotion she had seen from him. "Please forgive me; I—," she stammered.

"There is nothing to forgive in your quite natural reaction." The smile continued. "You see now why I hoped your brother would accompany my tour? I take great pleasure in hymn-singing, but it must be indulged in only under the harmony from a large congregation." Then the smile broke into a deep chuckle considerably more melodious than his singing, and Ned and Catherine joined in the laughter.

At last Ned spoke. "Catherine, I see I've taken on a much greater challenge than I realized. I fear I shall need help. I doubt the ability of even a great congregation to drown out this fellow's caterwauling. Won't you come with me on his tour? It would be a shame if all the potential hearers of the Word in Kent were to be scared off by the hymn-singing."

"Oh, Ned, I'd love to!" Her reaction was instinctive before common sense took over. "But, alas, I fear it's impossible. I mustn't leave my school duties, and we can't both abandon Durial." And then fear replaced common sense. "No, I really couldn't. So far on horseback . . ."

Ned put an understanding hand on her shoulder. "We could take the carriage, my dear. As to the school, couldn't Miss Owen oversee your students for just two weeks? And I've been thinking that our sister Elizabeth would be happy of an excuse to be closer to the London Society. She could stay with Durial."

Catherine laughed in spite of her concerns. "My, how efficient you are. But perhaps Mr. Ferrar does not want his tour so invaded."

Philip gave one of his small, stiff bows, which made the white Geneva bands at his neck fall forward from his black coat. "On the contrary, I would be very honored to have your company, Miss Perronet." And in spite of his stiffness, his eyes twinkled. "Besides, your brother is sure to need all the help he can get."

"We shall consider the matter further," Catherine said. She turned again to the keyboard where she played a brief melody before stopping to ask, "And have you a new hymn for us to try out, Ned?"

"Not yet ready to show even to so select a company, I fear. I have an image that seems stuck in my head every time I try to write, but I haven't succeeded in putting it in words. I see Christ on a great white throne with angels kneeling around Him, each one offering a crown and praising the power of His name. But the wording eludes me. I want to write a hymn of regal power and dignity that will bring honor to His majesty. I pray I will be worthy of the task."

"That is the prayer of each of us, is it not? To be worthy of our task." Catherine rose from the harpsichord bench and joined her brother in bidding their guest good night.

Later, alone in her room, the side curtains of her bed drawing her into her own little world, Catherine pondered Ned's parting remarks to her: "Do come with us, Cath. You need a change of scenery. It will take your mind off more painful things. And you can do some real good."

Catherine doubted just how much actual good she could accomplish. It seemed to her that the female members of the Society accompanied the preachers more for their own enlightenment or amusement—or for more subtle purposes, as she suspected of Grace Murray who often traveled with John Wesley. But then she scolded herself for being unfair. Women Society members counseled the women seekers in matters about which men would have no knowledge.

She had almost decided in favor of going when the vision of a large bay horse loomed, snorting, before her. She cowered into her pillows. *What utter nonsense . . . I should be ashamed . . .* Unthinkingly, she rubbed her fingers over her left collarbone and felt the sharp dip there. The imaginary horse snorted again, and the remembered pain in her shoulder was lost in the cries of her little brother who had toddled too close to the stamping feet.

But that was years ago. The crazed horse had been put down, her shoulder rarely ached anymore, and a rambling rose grew over the grave of little David in the Shoreham churchyard. She had overcome her fear sufficiently to ride when the occasion absolutely demanded it, but her greatest victory had been in becoming an expert driver.

So if they could take the carriage, and Elizabeth could stay with Durial, and Silas Told would allow Miss Owen to take her classes . . . She must admit there was something that appealed to her in the idea of helping Ned's strangely aloof colleague. As Ned had said after Philip left that evening, "We're not exactly friends. I certainly like him well enough. He's a fine fellow—don't know that I ever met better—but one can't get close enough to him to feel free to use the word *friend*." Yes, it might be worth knowing what was on the other side of that wall Philip Ferrar had erected around himself.

Three days later as the carriage rolled eastward along the old Roman road through the green countryside below the Thames, Catherine was glad of her decision. Whatever else might come of the journey, Ned's promise of a change of scene had been gloriously fulfilled. Hedgerows in new leaf sprouted buds that promised busy jam-making in cottage kitchens this summer; and rich, brown earth, yielding to the farmer's plow, would in a month or two show equal promise for a joyous fall Harvest Home festival. The fact that few trees had advanced past the bud stage did not daunt the flocks of chirping birds building their nests.

"Oh, Ned, just listen to that chorus," Catherine said to her brother beside her on the carriage seat. "Surely that will inspire your hymn-writing."

"Pardon?" He looked up absently from his paper.

"What poor company you make. You are far too busy listening to the tunes in your head to attend either to your sister or to nature's choristers. I find you quite hopeless."

"Philip!" Edward called to the rider just ahead of the carriage. "You must help me. My sister complains of my company, and I find her incessant chattering an intolerable interruption. Give me your horse."

"Incessant chattering! Sir, I protest. It was the second line I spoke to you in the better part of an hour. And how, pray tell, do you think to go on with your work on horseback?"

"I shall go on very well. Charles Wesley composes nearly all his hymns on horseback; he says the pace of the horse aids his sense of stately rhythm."

"Yes." Catherine guided Old Biggin around a mudhole left by recent rains. "And John Wesley gives all his attention to reading while on horseback. And they are both famous for their continual riding disasters because they never attend to their mounts. This time you're sure to break your arm, and then what will Durial say?"

But soon Philip was sitting beside her on the carriage seat while Ned, his reins looped across the saddle, followed at a distance. Here was her chance to get acquainted with the enigmatic man beside her, but her reticence took over, and she could think of nothing to say that didn't seem prying. So despite her denouncement as a chatterbox, it was Philip who broke the silence. "I am pleased you chose to come, Miss Perronet."

"Yes, I am too. But you must call me Catherine. Being traveling companions is almost like being family members."

"I would be honored—to use your name and to be so considered. You have a large family, I believe?"

Well, if she couldn't ask him about himself, she could tell him about herself; then maybe he would feel comfortable to be more open. "There were an even dozen of us, Mr. Ferrar."

"No, no. That will never do. If I am to call you Catherine,

you must call me Philip. Would you call your brother Mr. Perronet?"

"No, I wouldn't—Philip."

"There. Now, tell me more of your family."

"I shall do so, but you must absolve me of all accusations of chattering."

He raised his hand in a gesture of absolution.

"Well, Ned was always my favorite brother. With twelve children in the family it would be easy to get lost, to be just one of a crowd, but I was never that to Ned. He taught me to climb trees, helped me with my sums—which were always so easy for him and so impossible for me. He took me on long walks in the woods and taught me the names of the birds and flowers. I still keep my scrapbook of pressed flowers and hope to gather some new specimens on this trip."

She paused to observe the clumps of violets growing along the road.

"Ned encouraged my music when I became disheartened. Later I was able to return the favor by sharing the excitement over his compositions, and usually I'm the first to play one of his new hymns." She felt Philip's urging to continue her story.

"Little Charl was always my special charge, like I was Ned's. I suppose that's the way it works in all big families—each one looking out for the next younger. At least, that's how we did it. Anyway, Charl needed all the attention I could give him. He was forever wandering off and getting lost, getting hung up on a blackberry bush, or losing a boot in the mud. And it was my job to rescue him. Most of the time I didn't mind even if it did interrupt my reading.

"I suppose I was bred for Methodist Society work even before there was such a thing, because from my earliest memories I accompanied Mother when she visited the sick and needy in Papa's parish every week. Tuesday, Thursday, and Saturday were her regular visiting days, and at least three of us children always went with her, carrying baskets of garden vegetables, a fresh cheese, or herbs from the woods—whatever we had at hand or something she knew was needed.

"Dudy and Ned and I, or whoever accompanied her on that day, would occupy the children in the home so Mother could minister to the adults. Then we all joined in prayer before we left—or sometimes in song, especially when Ned was with us. His beautiful voice always made people feel better. I suppose that was one of the reasons—" She stopped abruptly, thankful for the lurch of the carriage that made the interruption seem natural. She had felt so at ease talking to Philip she had almost said that one of the reasons she loved Charles Wesley was that his was the only other voice she'd ever heard that was as sweet as her brother's.

"Yes?"

"So working with children has been my life since I was old enough to walk and talk. I've always loved it, and I can't imagine doing anything else.

"Gracious, I've talked an alarming distance. You must tell me of yourself now, er, Philip. What of your family?"

His level gaze that had so encouraged her comfortable reminiscences withdrew, and she felt as if the tremulous April sunshine had gone behind a cloud. Throughout her narrative he had leaned toward her, focusing on every word; but now he sat stiffly upright and looked straight ahead. It was obvious she had put a foot wrong. "Forgive me if I trespass. I—"

For a moment she thought she saw a flicker of emotion on his stoic features. "No, you have a right to know. I see now my error in not telling your brother. He would not have wanted his sister exposed—"

Before she could press him to complete his muddled remarks, Edward rode alongside them.

"How is it progressing, Ned?" Catherine asked.

"I don't know. I'm working on the phrase, 'All praise the name of Jesus.' It's the right idea, but it doesn't quite sing. I came to ask if Philip thought we should put up at the next village. The sky seems to be darkening rapidly."

Philip looked at the sky. "I had hoped to reach Rochester tonight and preach there in the morning before going on, but perhaps we could stop at Cobham if the inn is suitable for your sister's comfort."

Both men looked questioningly at Catherine, but she made no response. "What do you think, Cath?" Edward asked.

"*Hail*, I think."

Ned looked at the dark sky. "Perhaps, but I think rain more likely."

"Have you taken leave of your senses? *Reign* wouldn't suit at all. No wonder you're having trouble with your song."

"Catherine—I'm not talking about my writing. Philip and I want to know if you wish to put up at the nearest inn. It looks like rain coming."

"Oh, I daresay. Do as you think best. But try 'All hail the name of Jesus' in your song."

By the time they reached Cobham, the hypothetical rain had become a drenching reality. Travelers and horses didn't question the advisability of stopping at the inn, disreputable though it looked.

"I do apologize, Miss Perronet. You should never have been brought to such a place." Philip stood just inside the door surveying the dingy interior.

"Catherine," she reminded him firmly. "And do not worry yourself over the accommodation. I chose to come, and I shall make do with what presents itself."

But her brave words met a severe test when, after a brief washing in her damp-smelling room, she joined the men in the inn's only parlor. The room was crowded with ill-clad, unwashed villagers all talking in voices clearly emboldened by ale. "This is intolerable," Edward declared and strode off in search of the innkeeper.

"Catherine—" Philip took a step toward her.

"Mind your head!" The sharp crack told her that the warning came too late as Philip struck the low, blackened ceiling beam.

He rubbed his forehead ruefully. "You'd think one of my height would learn."

Ned joined them. "I gave orders for our supper to be served in my room. Its cramped condition will be preferable to this."

Indeed, Ned's small room, even with the fireplace that refused to draw properly, was an improvement, but the food set before them by a slatternly serving wench couldn't have been worse. The pools of fat floating on the stew had congealed into a stiff, white crust by the time it reached them. Even after Catherine pushed the fat aside and found a piece of meat, it was too tough to chew.

Ned took a bite of the bread. After no more than three chews, he grabbed for his cider mug and choked down a swallow of the sour liquid. "I advise you to avoid the bread." He wiped his mouth with the back of his hand, as no napkins had been provided. "In this dismal light I failed to see the mold on it, but the taste was unmistakable."

Philip chewed stoically on the rubbery meat and soggy vegetables. Then, after a sip of cider, he remarked, "It's no worse than the orphan asylum. Quite like, if my memory holds."

"Orphanage?" Catherine's fork hit her wooden serving trencher with a clatter.

Philip nodded without expression. "I started to tell you this afternoon. But I think it best to present you both with the full details now. Then if you wish to turn back in the morning, I shall understand."

"Turn back?" Catherine began, but her question was ignored as Philip turned to her brother.

"Edward, please believe that on my honor as a Christian I

would not have embarked on this journey had I realized the harm it could do to your sister's reputation."

"Nonsense. I am sufficient chaperone for her good name. Such travels are common practice."

"But not in the company of one with my background. I wish you to know the plain facts. I am a foundling."

There was no reply.

"An abandoned foundling. Which can mean only that my mother was a servant girl, or worse, and my father a care-for-nothing nobleman or a rake. Whatever the case may have been, the fact remains that, except at the very highest and lowest extremes of society, foundling means bastard and therefore disgrace. I know you will not want to expose your sister to such company."

Catherine broke in before Ned could reply, "What contemptible rubbish! I'll hear no more of it, sir, and neither will my brother."

Ned was thoughtful for a moment as the rain washed against the windows in great unremitting waves and the weak flame fluttered on the grate. Finally he spoke. "God has accepted you. With Him as your Father, there can be no more to say on the matter."

"You are very kind, Edward. But your sister—"

"My sister has spoken for herself most adequately."

"Both now and at some length this afternoon when I related my childhood to you. I think you should reciprocate, unless to do so would cause you pain." Catherine truly wanted to hear more of his history and felt in no hurry to leave even so small a comfort as Ned's weak fire for the chill dreariness of her own room.

"The subject is not at all painful to me," Philip assured her. "I simply fear disgusting others."

"Then be at rest, Philip. Ned is quite right. We share the same Father, so we are of the same family. There is no offense possible."

Philip nodded and stared into the fire. "I always took some comfort in the fact that Mrs. Ortlund found a remarkably clean and well-cared-for infant on her doorstep in the rush basket. It was most unusual, for a foundling often had little more than a few rags to protect it from the chill fog."

"Mrs. Ortlund raised you?" Catherine asked.

Again Philip nodded without looking at her. "She named me for a brother who died young. She had been a nurse at the Royal Asylum of St. Anne for Children Whose Parents Had Seen Better Days. The institution was no longer operating by the time I made my unwanted appearance into the world. But she ran a small asylum from the goodness of her heart and her own small living."

The wind and rain that whipped at the old inn made the three occupants of the room draw closer together. "I have never ceased to give thanks for Mrs. Ortlund. Were it not for her, I should have been sent to the parish poorhouse where it is unlikely I would have seen my first year through, amidst the filth, disease, and starvation."

Catherine shuddered.

"I have visited such places as an adult. Pandemonium and vice rule jointly among the paupers, fallen women, neglected children, vagrants, lunatics, aged, and ill. Had the usual fate befallen me, I should have been put in such a place where the best I could have hoped for was that some feeble crone might choose to care for a mewling infant for the short time it could be expected to survive."

"Were there no parish nurses?"

"Yes, but many were as lethal as the parish workhouse. Some are even called 'killing nurses.' More than three-fourths of the infants cared for by parish nurses die every year. I have looked into the subject with some interest. It seems that parish nurses who continue to bury infants week after week, with no criticism and no lessening of the number of children given them, take the hint. Society considers it very fit and convenient that such a child should die. After all, it relieves society of the care of an object that at worst is loathed and at best ignored. I thank God that by the large part of such society I was ignored."

All was silent in the room save for the incessant pounding of the rain. Then a violent gust of wind rattled the window panes so sharply that the three started. Catherine rose and smoothed her muslin skirt over its quilted petticoat. "It's past time we were in bed. Do you plan to preach in the fields at five in the morning as Mr. Wesley does?"

"I often do. It's a good idea to give the workers the Word of God before they begin their labors. But I fear we would have few hearers in the morning, even if the storm has passed. Let us rise at five and go on to Rochester for our first meeting. There is a small but faithful Society there."

"I will light you to your room." Ned picked up a candlestick.

Philip's room was next to Edward's, and when he opened the door, Catherine could see that his fire had gone out. She started toward the stairs and then turned back to say good night. In the frame of the dark doorway Philip looked remote and lonely. For a moment she felt she couldn't leave him like that. She took a step toward him.

"Cath!" Ned called impatiently from the stairway. She gave Philip a last small smile and rushed to her brother.

Philip watched Catherine fly up the stairs with a detachment that persisted from his orphanage days. He had learned early that it didn't pay to get too attached to people or things. People moved—went on to school or work; things were lost or stolen. He remembered the one thing that had been truly his, the blanket Mrs. Ortlund found him in. He had always kept it carefully folded in the bottom of the chest under his bed in the orphanage. But one day he returned from chapel to find the contents of the trunk spilled on his bed and the blanket gone. He hadn't even reported the incident, as the knowledge that he attached any importance to a worn, faded baby blanket would have made him a laughingstock.

His most determined efforts at detachment had failed him in one tender matter, however—the matter of Sally Gwynne. It was his own fault. He had broken his rule.

It happened without any rational awareness on his part. Indeed, until word reached him and other workers that day at the Foundery that Charles Wesley and Sally Gwynne were wed, he had had no understanding of the depth of his feeling. The fact that every young Methodist who preached in Wales or met Sally when she visited the Foundery with her father was more than half in love with the beautiful Welsh girl was no comfort to Philip. Nor did the fact that he would never have made an attempt to win her affections—nor have stood a chance had he done so—lessen the intensity of his feelings.

The cut was much sharper, although less deep, than the severing from his curacy had been. But both had produced the same results—an increased determination to remain aloof.

He turned to see if he could fan the few sparks on his grate into life. Then he saw his bag open on the floor. While he was next door in Ned's room, a thief had been at work here. His two leather-bound books and a linen shirt would fetch a few shillings when resold. Fortunately he always kept his purse with him, and he had little else of value to steal.

Gathering up his scattered goods brought to mind the theft in the orphanage and reminded him yet again of the rightness of forming no affections for things or people. There must be nothing in his heart worth stealing either.

3

*P*reachin' in the cockpit! Preachin' in the cockpit!" Two urchins ran through Rochester the next morning publicizing the meeting. And in the amphitheater usually used for much rougher purposes, the hymn-singing of a curious crowd attracted newcomers willing to stand in the drizzling rain for a fresh entertainment.

Catherine walked among the women on the edges of the crowd, welcoming them, helping them with their children, urging them to join in the singing, and ignoring the rude suggestions of two young ruffians who made no attempt to hide the bottles in their coat pockets.

The faithful of the Rochester Methodist Society sang loudly so that those unfamiliar with the songs could follow them. One of the members had requested permission to share his testimony. He took his place in the center of the ring, standing staunchly in spite of the jeers of the crowd.

"Need a drink, Buddy?"

"Haven't seen you at the inn lately; religion got you down?"

"Hey, Barber Bolton, how about a shave and a haircut—for a swig of gin?"

Bolton's voice rang above his rowdy audience. "I praise

God. When Mr. Wesley were at Rochester last, I were one of the most eminent drunkards in all the town—"

Cries of "'S truth" and "Don't we know it!" and "Miss the old times, Charlie?" interrupted him, but they subsided, and Bolton continued.

"Mr. Wesley was a-preachin' at the church. I come to listen at the window, and God struck me to the 'eart. I prayed for power against drinking. And God gave me more than I asked; 'e took away the very desire of it."

An egg flew through the air and landed at the speaker's feet. "Run 'em all out of town! They'll ruin business."

Bolton held up his hand. "Yet I felt myself worse and worse, till on April 25 last I could 'old out no longer. I knew I must drop into 'ell that moment unless God appeared to save me. And 'e did appear. I knew 'e loved me, and I felt sweet peace. Yet I did not dare to say I had faith—till yesterday was twelvemonth. God gave me faith, and 'is love 'as ever since filled my 'eart."

A combination of "amens" and jeers followed the speech, but then the audience became unusually quiet as Philip rose to preach. Catherine breathed a prayer that the service might continue without disruption.

Philip opened his Bible and began to read, "For by grace are—"

A loud squawking came from the back of the crowd, and the way parted for two men, each carrying a flapping, screeching rooster toward the center of the cockpit ring. "Now, me fine lords 'n ladies, as so many of you are gathered 'ere a'ready, we'll give you some *real* entertainment. On this side, Chanticleer, my fine red Pyle, and on t'other, Acey Jones's Wednesbury Grey. Fine fightin' cocks both in prime form. Who'll lay odds as to which of these fair-feathered fighters will be first to draw blood?"

Many in the audience surged forward to place bets. Philip turned to Ned. "Sing loudly and follow me." Holding his Bible aloft like a banner, Philip led the way through the mob, Ned and

Catherine behind him singing the Isaac Watts hymn, "We're Marching to Zion."

A vast number of people followed in parade to the market cross in the center of town, and more joined them along the way. Catherine hoped that now the chaff had been separated from the wheat and Philip would have receptive hearers. But as soon as he mounted the steps of the cross, the crowd began thrusting to and fro, and Philip was knocked from his perch on the highest stone step. Catherine started to cry out for fear he had been seriously hurt, but she saw him rise quickly and remount the steps.

The audience continued to shove, but Philip held his back firm against the stone cross and continued his Bible-reading. "'For by grace are ye saved through faith; and . . .'" Seeing they could not dislodge the preacher by pushing, those who had come for sport—considering field preachers fair game—began throwing stones. At the same time, some got up on the cross behind Philip to push him down. One man began shouting in his ear, making it impossible to continue the Scripture reading. Suddenly the tone of the shout changed to one of pain, and the man fell at Philip's feet, his cheek bleeding profusely where a stone intended for Philip had struck.

Then a second troublemaker, far more burly than the first, forced his way toward Philip. Before he could reach the cross though, a misdirected stone hit him on the forehead and bounced off. Blood ran down his face, and he advanced no farther.

A third reached out to grab Philip from the left. But a sharp stone aimed at Philip struck the attacker's fingers. With a howl of pain, the man dropped his hand and then stood silent. As if following his cue, the others became silent. Philip continued, "'By grace are ye saved through faith.' These two little words, faith and salvation, include the substance of all the Bible, the marrow, as it were, of the whole Scripture."

Catherine couldn't believe the change that came over

Philip as he spoke to the vast audience before him. Even in the press of the crowd when she had feared for his life, she had detected no change in his face, no show of emotion. But now his features took on a glow—an intense shine of joy that she would not have thought possible. And his voice—always so controlled, so evenly modulated, so devoid of any betraying feeling—now rang with the passion for truth. She felt as if she could see the Savior whom he proclaimed.

"And what is this faith through which we are saved? The Scripture speaks of it as a light, as a power of discerning. So St. Paul says, 'For God, who commanded the light to shine out of darkness, hath shined in our hearts, to give the light of the knowledge of the glory of God in the face of Jesus Christ.'"

As he spoke, the rain, which had been lessening for some time, stopped altogether; the clouds parted, and a shaft of sunlight fell on the fair-haired speaker standing on the market cross. His black cassock fluttered in the breeze, and his white satin surplice, remarkably unmuddied from the treatment he had received, gleamed in the sun.

"Faith is a divine evidence and conviction, not only that God was in Christ, reconciling the world unto Himself, but also that the Christ loved me and gave Himself for me. It is by this faith that we receive Christ . . ."

Catherine was so caught up by the preacher and his ringing words that for a moment she lost awareness of the people around her. Then she felt a sharp tug on her sleeve and turned to the woman beside her. "Sister, will ye pray with me? I 'ave need of such a faith."

Catherine led the seeker to the side of the crowd where they both bowed their heads. Catherine prayed first, then the woman. When Catherine looked up, she saw tears running down the woman's wrinkled, weather-beaten face. "Bless you, Sister; I've often 'eard these Methodists at their 'ymn-singing and wanted to join them, but I didn't know how. Now I've got a 'ymn-sing a-goin' in my 'eart."

Catherine introduced the new convert to a local Society member and turned to another who appeared to be seeking. "Would you like me to pray with you?" Perhaps twenty hungry souls were seeking the Savior around the old stone market cross.

A rough voice interrupted Catherine's prayer. She looked up, expecting more rabble, and a surprising sight met her eyes. A man in ragged, dirty clothes with greasy, matted hair hanging beneath a disreputable hat was holding a crisp white linen shirt aloft in one hand and two leather-bound books in the other. "I knowed it was a preacher cove I burgled in the inn last night when I seed 'is Bible an' preacher's garb. But I took w'at I could anyway. I was on my way to sell it for w'at I could w'en 'is words struck me to 'eart. 'Ere's yer swag, Mister. I repent a' me wicked ways."

Philip placed a hand on the man's shoulder. "I'll take the books as I doubt you have use for reading material. But you keep the shirt; you need it worse than I. Let it remind you of the new heart Christ has given you."

A chorus of "amens" and "praise the Lords" rose from the believers, turning to calls of "farewell" and "God go wi' thee" as Philip and the Perronets continued their journey.

From the carriage, Philip looked back at what was left of the congregation with open longing in his eyes. "It is always the same—the wrench at leaving new babes in the faith. How I long to stay among them! I believe this preaching like an apostle, without joining together those that are awakened and training them up in the ways of God, is only begetting children for the devil to steal. How much preaching has there been for ten years all over England! But where there is no regular preacher, no discipline, no order or connection, the consequence is that nine in ten of the once-awakened are now faster asleep than ever."

"The Society members—," Catherine began.

"Will do what they can to encourage one another in the faith, of course. But these people need a shepherd. What hope is there for such as that thief to build a new life without firm guidance?"

"The parish vicar?" Catherine tried again.

"Undoubtedly the holder of at least six livings who visits here once yearly as required by law in order to keep his income. What counsel exists is in the hands of a curate who, without the supervision of his superior, may be as lazy or drunken as suits him."

"Surely you exaggerate. My father—"

"Is a rare example of a godly man. One whose work I would emulate if a place were open to me."

"I understand you were formerly a curate . . ." Her sentence went unfinished as Old Biggin slipped in the deep mud. Ned drew alongside his sister. "We are nearly to the Medway. I think I should drive across. The waters are sure to be full and swift after the downpour."

The men changed places, and in a few minutes they approached the raised earthen causeway of ancient Roman construction. At least, that was where the crossing should have been. It was invisible under the rushing waters. "Can we ride the causeway?" Ned asked the ferryman.

"Yes, sir, if you keep in the middle."

Ahead of them, Philip urged his mount to cross the swollen stream. Obedient to her master's voice, Jezreel led the way into the water. Catherine held her breath, determined to remain calm.

Crossing with the carriage was more difficult. The water rose above the horses' knees and came to the bottom of the carriage. Catherine could feel the current pushing and sucking at the wheels to pull the vehicle sideways. She gripped the seat as Ned urged Biggin forward. "Easy, old boy. One step at a time. 'Atta boy. Keep going."

Just past the middle a swirl of water rushed over the causeway with the swiftness of a sluice. Catherine gave a cry of alarm as she saw Jezreel ahead of them lose her footing. But the horse gave a spring and recovered the roadway. With two final lunges, she scrambled up the eastern bank.

Biggin, older, and less agile than Philip's mare, was not so lucky. A few feet from shore his right forefoot slipped off the ramp. The carriage jolted as the horse fought to regain his footing. He couldn't find a hold in the muddy swirl. He swam valiantly, his heavily muscled thighs straining against the downstream rush.

The carriage, already nearly afloat in the deep water, tilted dangerously, then righted itself, and rode the tide behind Old Biggin. Catherine, soaked to her knees in the icy flood, gripped the seat as Ned fought to guide his horse. She tried to pray, but holding on took all her concentration.

Philip shouted to a group of men on the bank waiting for the ferry. Forming two rows of human pulleys, they reached out with strong hands for each side of Biggin's harness as he neared shore. The first man missed his grab at the wet leather, but the second grasped it firmly. Straining, they pulled the heaving horse up the miry bank.

Catherine took in a great gulp of air and started to relax when a grating crunch of metal on stone rent the air. The carriage wheel on Ned's side had struck a boulder half-buried in the mud. For a moment the vehicle balanced on one wheel. Then it toppled on its side, spilling passengers and luggage into the mud and water.

The world blurred and darkened. Catherine felt her hands slide through the slimy brown ooze of the river bank. She smelled the heavy, wet earth. She slid toward the raging waters, her wet, heavy skirts pulling her downward. She screamed and clawed at the slimy bank.

Just as the cold grasp of the river tugged at her feet, a strong hand encircled her flailing arm. Philip, supported by two burly river men, pulled her from the clutches of the water. In a few moments she was on top of the bank.

The men unhitched Biggin and retrieved the suitcases

from the muck. Ned, Catherine, and Philip sat down on tree stumps above the river to survey the wreckage.

"Compared to what I feared when I saw your carriage go into the water, I cannot regard the broken axle as a disaster," Philip said. He turned toward Catherine, but he said nothing more.

Trembling, she reached out to him, disregarding the mud covering them both. "You saved my life."

Ned put his arm around his shivering sister. "We are much indebted to you, Philip. We are indeed fortunate. Neither of us nor Biggin is hurt, and only one bag is lost in the river."

"It's easy for you to say 'only one,' considering it was my case." Catherine forced a lightness as she regarded her muddy gown and thought of her belongings swirling away down river.

"Chatham is just ahead. You can purchase some necessities there while Philip and I arrange to have the carriage repaired and hire a chaise for the rest of the journey."

"Hire a chaise?" Catherine wiped a sodden curl away from her cheek and tried to sound casual. "What nonsensical extravagance, Brother. You would be far better served to purchase a saddle for Biggin." She forced a smile that showed by its very brilliance how terrified she was. The other Methodist sisters rode pillion on circuit. She could do it too. It was high time she laid her fear to rest.

"But, Cath—" Ned tightened his arm encircling her shoulder. "That would mean you must ride pillion. I can afford to hire—"

"No. No chaise." The words were firm but were followed by a small gulp. "I'll be all right. There must be an inn up the road where we can dry out and get warm."

"Cath," Ned tried again.

"I'll be fine." Her insistence was more for her own benefit than for her companions'. To give action to her words she stood and began walking up the road. Without thinking about it, she put a hand on her left shoulder. The cold, wet weather had made the injury ache, as it often did, and brought the old experience vividly alive to her . . . The big bay horse lowering his head and lashing out with his hind feet, then rearing in front, and landing stiff-legged with a jolt that jarred her teeth. The helpless, sick feeling of slipping, at first slowly, then faster and faster, and plunging to the hard earth. The blowing snort from the horse, the cry from her baby brother, and then silence as the pain in her shoulder brought the blessed oblivion of unconsciousness. When she woke, they told her about David.

She never saw the horse again nor her brother. She had probably ridden only ten or twelve times in her life since then, and never pillion. Could she do it now? The answer was there as soon as the question formed: "I can do all things through Christ which strengtheneth me." She gave her shoulder a final rub as she pulled a foot from the mud and set it on the path before her.

The inn they found was a considerable improvement on the one they had stayed in the night before. As the hour was late by the time Ned completed arrangements for the carriage and they were wet and cold, they decided to stay the night.

The next morning the travelers continued their journey to the accompaniment of the dawn chorus. Since Old Biggin, for all his gentleness, was not really a saddle horse, they decided it would be better to tie their cases on behind Ned and have Catherine ride pillion on Jezreel. Catherine accused her brother of caring more for his privacy than her comfort, and he replied that she had already informed him of her opinion of his companionship, thank you. In this spirit of raillery, Catherine covered her fears as Ned made a stirrup of his hands and tossed her onto the blanket behind Philip.

Sitting sidesaddle, she smoothed her round skirt over her petticoat and placed her left arm loosely around Philip's waist. "Are you all right?" he asked. "Ned told me of your accident. If I can do anything to make you more comfortable—"

"I thank you for your thoughtfulness, but I assure you I am quite all right."

"Very well. But if at any time you wish me to stop or ease the pace, please say so at once."

Catherine appreciated his concern, but she was determined to conquer her fear. Besides, with this stalwart man in the saddle and the birds singing them on their way in the fresh spring air, riding didn't seem so frightful. Even so, she had an idea that it might be well to occupy her mind with conversation.

So a few minutes later when a gentle mist fell on them through the lightly-leaved trees that arched over the road toward Canterbury, Catherine was reminded of a line from Chaucer. She began quoting, "'When the sweet rains of April fall, they of England to Canterbury wend.' If the rains in Chaucer's time were anything like yesterday, that is surely one of the greatest understatements in the language. Might as well call Noah's forty days and nights of deluge 'sweet rains.'"

"We are not far north of the Pilgrim's Way. The road Chaucer's pilgrims took is still in use," Philip said.

"As well as the road the murderers from Henry's court would have taken to slay Thomas à Becket?"

They talked for a while of the Archbishop whose martyrdom had turned Canterbury Cathedral into the most popular pilgrimage shrine of the Middle Ages and of Chaucer who had immortalized the journey. Then the topic seemed to pall, and Catherine sought another to occupy her mind. "Before our misadventures yesterday, I believe you were about to tell me of your curacy."

The back before her stiffened slightly, and she wondered how she could have given offense. Then the wide shoulders squared. "I don't know what I was about to tell you, but my brief curacy in Midhurst was a poor living. Yet it gave me the feeling of having come home. I thought it was the place God had prepared for me and that I would be there forever, serving Him and those people—belonging to them.

"Forever lasted almost two years. Until the second time the vicar, on his yearly round of visits to his several livings, heard that his curate was an enthusiast who preached a personal salvation from the pulpit, read the prayers with fervor, and had the effrontery to suggest that good Englishmen ask forgiveness for their sins.

"I was given the briefest of hearings and promptly replaced with a young Oxford graduate whom the vicar knew from his card parties."

His words were astringent, but Catherine, her sensitivities enhanced by the days of being so close to Philip and by having lost something dearly longed for herself, could hear between the lines. She knew that for the young man who had never truly belonged anywhere, those brief months had shown him that belonging was what he wanted most in life. She knew that they had provided an identity he lacked. And in the months since leaving Sussex, riding circuit, preaching with the band of Methodist ministers in fields or meetinghouses or wherever people would listen to him had satisfied his desire to share God's Word, but had in no way fulfilled his need to belong.

Indeed, she realized the desire had grown stronger, as she had witnessed at Rochester. Each time he would meet new people, new converts would come into the fold, and a new Society would be established; then Philip would have to ride away, leaving the people. He longed to be a part of their lives. He wished to marry them, to christen their children, to bury their dead, to attend to all the daily needs of a flock—not just come into their lives for a day or a week and then ride out again.

He told her of the day he had left Midhurst, how little Jennie Franks came early in the morning with a drooping bunch of bluebells crushed in her childish hand. Catherine could see him accepting them gravely as the tribute they were intended to be. She could even see the corn-silk pigtails shining in the sun as he patted Jennie's head and the single tear that slipped from the corner of her eye just before she ran for home.

Jennie had been the first of a long string that morning—old Mrs. Machin with a loaf of fresh bread for his journey, Mrs.

Patching with a crock of pickled peaches, the Timmon sisters with a hand-worked altar cloth—which he had never had a place to use.

As Philip's crisp sentences matched Jezreel's gait, Catherine could see that string of loyal, taciturn people, each expressing their love in a tangible way, but without words. Her arm tightened ever so slightly around his thin waist as they rode in silence for several minutes. Then Catherine reached back and patted the shiny chestnut rump of their mount. "Jezreel's a good horse. It won't tire her too much carrying us both?"

Sitting behind Philip, she heard rather than saw his rare smile. "It would take a great deal more than your extra weight at this sedate pace to tire Jezreel. She is an excellent animal. I fear you've uncovered my one extravagance, but I'll admit to a great fondness for horses. I can't remember a time when I wasn't hoarding a small pile of farthings for 'my horse.' At least my curacy lasted long enough that I was able to add a few more shillings to my cache and accept farmer Brock's generous offer of sale. I've no doubt the animal could have fetched twice his price at market. Even then she is an extravagance for me. But I salve my conscience with the argument that nothing can be more important to a circuit-riding preacher than a good mount."

Again Catherine stroked the satiny horsehair. Somehow the information that Philip was fond of horses increased her determination to conquer her fear. Each mile she rode became a small victory.

They reached Sittingbourne in time for a late afternoon meeting in a green, tree-encircled meadow near the town. Their timing was perfect as the meeting attracted the laborers leaving the fields for their evening meal. Soon a crowd of several hundred had gathered. The rain ceased, and a gentle setting sun shone on the field. Catherine hoped the service would not be disrupted.

But Philip had no more than read his text when a raucous

shout began on the far side of the field. Several men were driving an ox into the congregation. It was impossible to preach, so Ned jumped up beside Philip on the low stone wall and started a hymn. The efforts of the disorderly were in vain, for the great white ox ran round and round the field, one way and the other, eluding the men's sticks. At length he broke through the midst of his drivers and loped off toward the woods, leaving the worshipers rejoicing and praising God.

The next day the service at Faversham met worse resistance. The Society there had arranged for the preaching to take place at a little meetinghouse, but the vast numbers who thronged to the service quickly overflowed the room. They moved a small wooden table into a nearby field, and Philip mounted it to preach. He had no more than begun when a young man rushed in, cursing and swearing vehemently. The people near him tried to make him leave.

"No, Brothers. Let him stay if he will agree to be quiet," Philip said. The curses subsided to a mutter, and Philip resumed preaching.

"Repentance means an inward change, a change of mind from sin to holiness, but first we must know ourselves sinners, yea, guilty, helpless sinners."

"That's no way to talk to respectable folk, Parson!" The shout came from a young man dressed as a gentleman but with oddly bulging pockets.

Another young man nearby cried, "Why, if it isn't my old mate, Bradford White!" He threw out his arms and embraced his friend, bulging pockets and all. Even from where Catherine stood some distance away, the cracking sound was audible. And then the air reeked of rotten eggs.

The crowd drew back from the pungent sulphur odor; women put handkerchiefs over their noses, and the young man, dripping a sticky yellow trail, beat a hasty retreat.

Philip had only begun again on his topic when a mob of ruffians rushed upon the crowd with a bull they had been baiting. They tried to drive him in among the people, but the beast continually dodged to one side and then the other.

The drivers saw that their sticks and goads were not going to succeed with the beast, so they tied ropes around his neck and dragged him through the people. By this time the poor animal was tired and bloody from having been beaten and torn by dogs and men. When its tormenters thrust it in front of Philip, the greatest danger was that the bull might bloody the preacher's cassock. More than once Philip put his hand out to thrust the poor creature's head away so the blood would not drip on his clothes.

But in the end, the rabble almost won the day. They so pressed the bull against the small table Philip was standing on that it began to rock dangerously. The bull moved away, but it was driven again against the table. This time there was the sound of splintering wood, and Philip, going down with his table, fell toward the horns of the bull.

Strong arms of those nearby grabbed Philip just in time. Defeated, the rabble trudged off, leading their bewildered bull behind them.

Philip found a small rise of ground where he could stand to finish his sermon. Ned again led in singing, and groups began praying all around the field that still bore spatters of rancid egg yolk and red drops of bull blood. Then yet another shout interrupted the prayers. This came from the man who had interrupted the service with shouts and curses early on, but now his tone was far different. He declared that he had been a smuggler and had his swag bag with him to prove his claim. "But I'll never do that no more. I'm resolved to 'ave the Lord for my God."

Even the exhilaration of a victorious service overcoming such obstacles, however, wasn't enough to sustain Catherine's spirits when she saw the night's lodging that had been provided for them by the poverty-stricken Society members. Her room was little better than a cellar. She had to go down three steps and duck her head through the doorway to enter. The initial sensation in the room was one of chill dampness. After some time of restless tossing, however, she realized the major obstacle to comfort and sleep was the stuffiness of the cramped quarters. Throwing off her covers, she groped her way across the room to where she could see the dim light of the moon shining against the waxed paper covering the window. She tore the paper from one of the panes and took a deep gulp of the fresh, sweet air now blowing through the opening.

Back in her bed, huddled under her covers, a strange new thought came over Catherine. If the near drownings, stonings, and bull-tramplings, followed by fatigue, starvation, and discomfort of the past days were typical of itinerant preaching, she certainly did not envy the former Miss Sally Gwynne. With a flash of humor and amazement, Catherine found herself pitying the young woman who was newly wed to one of the most active circuit-riding preachers in the Methodist Society. As she drifted off to sleep in her cryptlike room, Catherine wondered if her bitter disappointment had, in truth, been a blessed deliverance.

*I*t rained during the night, so on a washed and shining morning their little party set out on its last lap to Canterbury. Having accomplished one day of pillion riding without disaster, Catherine was now a little more at ease and still smiling over the Society member's parting admonition, "Don't get carried off by no Frenchies!" She sat in silence behind Philip as they rode through the bright green and gold morning.

She thought about her companion's silence—so still, so reticent—and yet she felt at peace in his company even without knowing him well. Perhaps it was because he was at peace with himself, if not with his circumstances.

After more time passed, she asked, "Have you always wanted to preach?" Her soft words matched the rhythm of Jezreel's hoofbeats.

"I had not thought to preach until I came really to understand the basis of my faith while at Cambridge. But from earliest memories I loved the church. Other boys at the foundling school complained about having to attend services, and at Cambridge my fellow gownsmen universally sneered at and slept through the twice-daily chapel. But I felt differently."

The taciturn Philip obviously found it difficult to speak of his feelings, and Catherine could only guess at all the words encompassed. Philip had loved the church for more reasons than the spiritual—the peace and beauty there satisfied an aesthetic need deep within him, which certainly nothing in the orphanage or his daily school life could fulfill. And something else, perhaps the sense of being near God—of belonging to Him—met his undefined need.

"The orphanage school was a good one?"

"An excellent school—strict and proper. Then I attended Cambridge as a Sizar." And again it was necessary for his listener to embroider between the spoken words to picture the training in cleanliness and manners far beyond what most boys of his class would have received at home and the well-grounded, if coldly formal, religious training to which his soul had responded with unaccustomed warmth. And at the university, this training supplied the discipline and humility required to fulfill his role as a servant to other students.

"At Cambridge you found assurance of your faith?"

He nodded. "Through reading the works of William Law. Long before that time, Law had been forced to leave Cambridge for refusing to take the oath of allegiance to George I. After I read his *Serious Call to a Devout and Holy Life*, I called on him for counsel."

"As did the Wesley brothers, I believe."

"Yes. Like so many others who read his excellent book and sought out its author, I found the assurance of my salvation." He had found there a place of belonging for his soul. But having his heart set on a heavenly home only increased his feelings of not belonging here. And grasping the warmth and comfort of that hitherto foreign word *home* only increased his undefined longing for an earthly home.

Suddenly the sound of pealing bells rang on the bright air, calling all who would to worship. Through the tree branches, past a field of new-sprouted grain, beyond the medieval stone wall and town buildings rose the triumphant square towers of Canterbury Cathedral.

As they rode along St. Peter's Place and then turned up High Street, the church grew before Catherine's fascinated gaze. She felt her excitement mounting. Here Christian worship had flourished since Roman times; here the Christian Queen Bertha and her ladies had faithfully prayed for the conversion of this island every day for forty years; here stood the Saxon font where Bertha's husband, the newly converted King Ethelbert of Kent, was baptized by St. Augustine on Whitsunday in 597, an act symbolizing the first official acceptance of Christianity in the Anglo-Saxon realms; here St. Augustine himself became the first Archbishop. Here was the mother church of English Christendom, the cradle of English Christianity.

And now Catherine would attend Sunday morning worship on the spot where Christian worship had been offered continuously for 1,150 years. They tethered the horses by the southwest porch and entered the magnificent perpendicular nave where Catherine's gaze was drawn up, up, up to the very heavens along with the prayers offered there daily to the glory of God. They took the seats the verger led them to in the choir, and Catherine thought of the Old Testament account of how the people under Solomon's direction had built the Temple of God. Here too at Canterbury the workmen had labored, as generation after generation of stone masons, glass-blowers, and wood-carvers plied their humble trades to express their faith.

Throughout the singing of the anthem, the praying of the collect, the reading of the Epistle and Gospel, the preaching of the sermon, the ministry of the sacrament, and the singing of the Gloria, Catherine kept thinking of how God had helped Solomon and all those in the Old and New Testaments to build and spread the faith, of how He had helped the Christians in England down through the ages. Surely He would help His people now who were doing His work. As she looked up the nave to the high altar and above to the ceiling with its pillars and arches spreading like a vast forest of trees with their branches entwined in prayer, she prayed that Philip would not be forced to leave his historic faith in order to minister. *Find him a place, Lord.* She breathed it over and over.

"Glory be to the Father and to the Son and to the Holy Ghost; as it was in the beginning, is now and ever shall be: world without end, amen." Catherine sang with the congregation and then knelt for the singing of the blessing.

After the service, Ned and Philip decided to climb the tower to the belfry to view Canterbury and the surrounding country-side. But Catherine preferred to make her own pilgrimage. She climbed a series of stairs to the highest level in the cathedral where for hundreds of years the shrine of St. Thomas had drawn the faithful. As she ascended each worn stone step, she took care to place her feet in the deepest of the hollows, stepping where centuries of devout travelers had worn the solid stone away with steps of devotion and penitence.

She was thankful for a faith that didn't rely for its assurance on such outward works, but she was also thankful for those faithful ones who were willing to do what they thought right. At the shrine she walked around the wide barren floor that had once supported Thomas à Becket's tomb. She remembered that the golden, gem-encrusted casket had been destroyed during the Reformation. Surely, Thomas himself would have preferred this powerful symbolism of the empty space left by a man's death. The thought moved her deeply. In a great cathedral of carved marble and jeweled stained-glass, what could better express the vacancy left by the death of a man who gave his life for his faith?

Thomas à Becket had built the cathedral with his death. His martyrdom had brought pilgrims from all over the world, and much of the splendor of architecture and decoration had come from the wealth brought by these pilgrims.

Suddenly overwhelmed, she whispered, "Thank You, Lord, that no matter how difficult it is for Philip and other Methodist ministers, they won't have to die as martyrs." They might be forced to preach in the fields, to live a life of itinerant hardship, even to sign the Act of Toleration and declare themselves dissenters, but at least there *was* an Act of Toleration. No longer were men put to death in England for their faith as St. Thomas was, or the Lollards, or any whose faith happened to disagree with the king's. King George II might have his faults, but he didn't behead those who disagreed with him.

Along the wall Catherine saw statues of great men of history kneeling in prayer—priests and bishops, as one would expect in a cathedral; but even more impressive, Catherine felt, were the generals, dukes, and ministers, the lords temporal who acknowledged their reliance on God as they made decisions and led armies that determined England's destiny.

She descended the stairs on the other side of the chapel, again feeling the swale in the stone made by both the great and the humble, in whose footsteps she walked. And she remembered a couplet John Wesley wrote after visiting a famous castle purported to be the most ancient building in England:

> A little pomp, a little sway,
> A sunbeam in a winter's day,
> Is all the great and mighty have
> Between the cradle and the grave.

Catherine, Edward, and Philip had just time to eat a light lunch before the service they were to hold for the Society John Wesley had founded and nurtured on his many visits to Canterbury. They left the city through the ancient Quenin Gate, and outside the wall they met a large number of Society members who had gathered to accompany them up the hill to St. Martin's Church.

Before they could reach the church, however, a crowd of rabble gathered, like flies to a honey sandwich. The troublemakers followed them up the hill through the grounds of St.

Augustine's ruined abbey, showering cups of water over the marchers. When that failed to dampen any spirits, they tossed lighted fireworks into the crowd. Fortunately, the water had wetted the ladies' skirts and caps and the men's coats so that no serious fires started. The procession speeded up, to the accompaniment of explosions and shrieks.

By the time they reached St. Martin's Church, the rabble had run out of weapons and lost interest. Undoubtedly the sight of several hundred soldiers in the congregation helped curb their enthusiasm. Canterbury hosted a major army garrison, situated as it was in a strategic position to guard the English Channel from invasion by England's ancient enemy, France. Indeed, since the recent French attempt to capture Minorca which, along with Gibraltar, gave England naval supremacy in the Mediterranean, Pitt's government was almost neurotic about a French attack. So of late the garrison numbers had been greatly increased. Wesley's services had always been well attended by red-coated soldiers, and many had been converted by his preaching.

The lusty male voices rang out as Edward led them in one of the hymns newly penned by Charles Wesley, "Oh, for a Heart to Praise My God." St. Martin's was far too small to hold all their hearers, but the square Saxon tower of stone and Roman brick made a backdrop like a high altar canopy, and the grave-covered hillside formed a natural amphitheater, with the fir trees spreading their branches overhead like the finest Gothic arches. Birdsong accompanied the singing, as more worshipers and curiosity-seekers made their way up the hill from town.

The crowd now settled down and entered wholeheartedly into the singing. Then they gave rapt attention to Philip's preaching. "If any of you lacks wisdom, let him ask God, who gives to all men generously . . ." Catherine thought of her own lack of wisdom and her own doubts. But instead of concentrating on the preacher's words, she found herself focusing on the preacher. The long nose with skin drawn tight over the cheekbones, the deep-set solemn eyes, the strong jaw line and squared-off chin—his features spoke of might and durability as clearly as the ancient stones around him. The preacher stretched out an arm, and a long, thin wrist bone extended beyond the white cuff of the shirt sleeve beneath his black cassock. Catherine found the gesture so appealing that she had to force her mind back to the words of Scripture Philip was quoting: "'I will instruct thee and teach thee in the way which thou shalt go; I will guide thee with mine eye . . .'"

Catherine prayed silently, *Father, please show me the way you want me to*—The rustle started so slowly she first thought it was the wind rising in the fir trees. Then it grew. Suddenly the disturbance moved through the whole congregation like wild-fire. "Landed at Dover?" "Less than an hour's march from Canterbury?" "Burning the fields!" A woman shrieked, "Lord, have mercy on us!"

The soldiers came to attention as a sergeant barked out orders. Civilians milled in the way, but in the best order possible, soldiers assembled for command. And everywhere rose the cry, "The French have landed!" "The French!" "It's the French—they're coming!"

Imperturbable, Philip shouted, "Don't panic. Keep calm. Just move toward your homes quickly and in order. And look to God." But pandemonium reigned. Catherine watched the flee-ing backs of people who moments ago had worshiped beside her.

"Do you think it's true?" she asked Ned. Her voice was calm, but her eyes were wide with apprehension.

"It's doubtful. Such alarms go around regularly, I'm told. More than likely the rumor was started by one of the rabble, since no army messenger arrived with a dispatch. In this part of Kent small children are taught obedience with the warning, 'And if you don't, the French will get you.'"

"But there *is* war on the continent these seven years past . . ." She hesitated, for to her "the French" meant Aunt

Nicola and a noisy family of cousins living on the Perronet family estate in Nyon; but France was also England's rival, and it was just possible . . .

Philip joined them. "All the more reason to suppose the French well occupied on the continent. But the fox is with the hens now—the story of an invasion will spread through the town, and tumult will reign for at least twenty-four hours. We may as well go on. There'll be no chance of holding another service for some time."

Back at the Chaucer Inn, Philip removed his cassock and replaced it with a black frock coat, close-fitting to the waist, with a flared skirt to knee level, its back and side vents making it comfortable for riding.

Each day's travel made Catherine miss her lost luggage more. She had purchased an ivory comb and a boar bristle brush and a few other items of absolute necessity, but chose to hold out until she reached Shoreham and her mother's dressmaker before replacing her wardrobe. She tied a full-length cotton apron over her gown to cover the worst of the spots and could only be thankful that the day of the accident she had been wearing the warmer of her two dresses and her long hooded mantle. Even if the rain returned, she would have some shelter. But that was her only comforting thought as they set out again on their journey. She had never traveled the road to Tunbridge Wells, the next town where a Society was awaiting them, but she knew it was a long ride and that the reception at the meetings along the way was unlikely to be friendly.

As they left Canterbury and rode into the lush green countryside of Kent, Catherine thought that surely this had to be the sweetest, greenest land God had ever smiled on. Fields of hops and wheat and vegetable gardens were beginning to green as April passed into May; fruit orchards showed promise of bloom; and the hawthorn tree, called the May tree by the poets, graced the landscape with its sweet spring blossoms. The sheep on the hillsides made Catherine think of the psalmist's words, "We are the sheep of His pasture." And here and there the pastoral scene was dotted with red brick tile-roofed farmhouses and round cone-roofed oast houses where the locally grown hops were dried for brewing.

They made one detour to spend the night at the farm owned by Vincent Perronet. The stone house was surrounded by rich, black soil and green pastures that fed the red-brown Guernsey cows. The land agent greeted the travelers warmly, and his wife served tea and parkin while Ned went over the account books. Catherine savored the heavy oatmeal spice cake sweetened with honey as she listened to Mrs. Adisham's gossip about the tenants and her own brood.

"Our Mary was the last to go. She married a ship's chandler over to Dover way. I'd like it right fine to go visit her when her first is born, but Adisham says he can't take me until after the harvest. And I says the child will like to be walking by then, and isn't it time he thought about taking it a little easier? His rheumatiz troubles him something fierce when the rains come on. But your father is the fairest of landlords, Miss Perronet, a right finer man to work for, there isn't."

When the refreshments were finished, Farmer Adisham conducted his guests on a tour around the farm. "They's good, hard-working tenants," he said pointing to a small cottage nestled in a clump of trees. "But you won't see much labor about today, not with the Maying." He indicated a group of milkmaids walking beside the road, boughs of pink-tinged hawthorn blossoms in their arms.

After taking leave of their guide, they rode through the village of Chartham. Suddenly the merry music of a fiddle and the sound of laughter came to their ears. Rounding the corner of a tavern, they saw the village green stretching before them. A maypole, fifty feet high, rose from the grass. Ribbons and garlands of flowers and greenery wound around the pole, the work of village young people shortly after sun-up that morning. And circling the pole danced a cluster of country revelers.

To one side sat the floral-crowned May Queen, the most beautiful girl in the village, chosen to represent summer and to preside over all the May celebrations. Near her the Jack-in-the-Green cavorted with a band of small children carrying flower-entwined hoops. He wore a heavy wicker cage completely covered with greenery so that only his eyes and feet were visible. On yet another part of the common, a band of Morris men in their white flower-and-ribbon-bedecked suits danced gaily to the rhythm of the bells attached to their ankles and the tune of the piper who led them.

Catherine's heart soared with delight at the beauty and carefree joy. How wonderful that England could celebrate May Day again. It was nearly a hundred years since the festival had been sternly outlawed by Cromwell's Puritans. Now it was again in full flower. She would have loved to spend the day there, but she knew they must go on.

With such happy scenes and the agreeable weather, the miles at first seemed to pass more quickly beneath their horses' plodding feet. But as mile after mile wore on, Catherine began to weary. The countryside was no less green and pleasant, but her capacity to appreciate it faded faster than the afternoon sun.

In all, it took five more days of wearisome pillion riding before they reached Tunbridge Wells. Catherine felt as if she had grown to Jezreel and wondered: if a mythological male with four horse's legs was a centaur, what was a female creature?

The hardest day was at Goudhurst. Catherine rose at four o'clock for private devotions; Philip held the first preaching service at five o'clock in a field. Wet with morning dew, Catherine was sure she and all the congregation would catch pneumonia. Then followed three more services throughout the day at neighboring villages, each with some share of rowdyism and of spiritual victory as well.

By that evening as they rode the last few miles to an inn, Catherine's head, shoulders, and back ached. She wondered if she'd ever feel good again. She did the only thing she could—

hang on and pray, "Help me to travel in Thy strength, O Lord. Thy strength which is made perfect in our weakness . . . and, O Lord, I am so weak."

Catherine was determined not to utter one word of complaint. And when Catherine Perronet was determined, she was very determined indeed.

She thought of Jesus sitting at the well of Samaria—"Jesus, therefore, being wearied with His journey . . ." And she prayed, "Yes, Lord, You do know how I feel. You were weary too." Some of the tenseness left her body, and before she knew it, she began singing Martin Luther's words: "Did we in our own strength confide, / Our striving would be losing, / Were not the right Man on our side, / The Man of God's own choosing. . . . Christ Jesus, it is He, . . . And He must win the battle."

Philip joined her on the last line. They were drawing near to an inn that promised nothing but poor food and a lumpy bed, but Catherine's spirits were revived.

As Philip followed Ned and Catherine into the inn, he suddenly realized that he was so tired he could hardly stand up. This had been one of the most demanding and draining days of his life. He was not unused to hard riding after little sleep, nor was he unaccustomed to facing large and hostile crowds; but he had never before had the additional burden—no, challenge—of responsibility for another. And although Edward was always nearby on Old Biggin, it was Philip who worried about Catherine's physical comfort and mental ease as she rode behind him.

In meetings he had always been concerned for the souls he spoke to and conscious of his responsibility to God. But over the past days, he had felt a new self-consciousness as he thought about Catherine being in the congregation. It disturbed him that it should be so, and the additional strain fatigued him.

In spite of the meanness of the inn, the landlord Crimpton

was able to provide a private parlor where the travelers could eat their brown bread, cabbage, and collops with eggs. As they sat near the fire that evening, Edward, as usual, bent over a book at a small table with a branched candelabra, leaving Catherine and Philip in a world of their own, talking softly by the fire. Perhaps because of their brief burst of duet that day, the conversation turned to hymns and hymn writers. Without giving any thought to her words, Catherine said, "Yes, I'm sure the beauty of Charles Wesley's hymns was the cause of much of my attraction—" She gave a small gasp as her hand flew to her mouth.

Philip leaned forward, his elbows on his knees, his level, solemn gaze focused on her. "That day we met at the Foundery, you had been praying in much agony of spirit."

She gave a tiny nod. "I had just heard of the marriage."

He nodded. "And I too."

"You too? . . . You mean, Sally?"

"She was very special. Of course I had no expectations . . ." He tried to keep his eyes free of any flicker of pain that might show how deep the wound had gone.

"So the refused curacy was not your only disappointment that day." Catherine put out her hand in a tentative gesture as if she would touch the creases at the corner of his sad eyes, then hesitated, and lowered her arm, her fingers just brushing the back of his hand.

But that brief touch, as light as a butterfly wing, was the most warming human contact he had known in a long time. The gentle friendliness of it went all through him.

They continued to sit for some time, the occasional crackling of a log the only sound in the room. Neither one moved, and yet it was as if they had drawn closer together.

At last Ned closed his book, blew out a guttering candle, stood, and stretched with noises that seemed raucous in the quiet of the room. "We must go to bed; we have a full day of riding to reach the Wells tomorrow."

As if to cover the telling intimacy of the quiet, Catherine

crossed to her brother with unaccustomed vivacity and gave him a good-night kiss upon the cheek. Ned, his arms still spread out in a stretch, enfolded her in a huge embrace. "Sleep well, Cath." He released her with a brotherly pat on the shoulder.

She turned in a flurry from Ned to Philip and became suddenly shy. She held out her hand. "Good night then." She fled from the room.

Philip was left alone in the suddenly empty parlor, trying to understand the strange emotion he felt. He hesitated to put a name on it since it seemed ludicrous, but . . . why should he feel jealousy at the closeness of brother and sister? What did such a scene have to do with him? Or was that the reason? He had never been part of such a scene.

*L*ate the next afternoon they arrived at Tunbridge Wells nestled in a valley of steep sandstone hills. The road into town led down the hill known as Mount Ephraim, the most fashionable residential section of the elegant city. Since the discovery of its mineral water wells in 1606, Tunbridge Wells had grown to be the chief resort of London intellectuals and was second only to Bath as the most popular watering place in England.

Sitting on their mounts, the three travelers watched elegantly clad strollers promenading beneath the grove of trees. The men were outfitted in coats of rich velvet and brocade, heavily embroidered on the wide cuffs turned up to the elbow. Their waistcoats displayed equally intricate needlework in silver and colored silks, with froths of lace at the neck and wrists. Most men wore braid or feather-trimmed tricorns atop their tie-back wigs or carefully powdered hair, but some coiffures were sufficiently complicated to make the wearing of a hat uncomfortable, so those gentlemen carried their hats under their arms.

And the powdered and pomaded ladies strolling on the arms of the gentlemen were dressed in sackback gowns of exquisite fabric fastened at the waist to reveal heavily embroidered stomachers, their V-shape meeting the embroidered petticoat flaring at the hips over an oblong hoop to emphasize the wearer's tiny waist. Triple flounces of lace finished the sleeves which ended at the elbow; lace caps showed beneath the wide-brimmed Bergere hats.

Catherine thought it one of the prettiest scenes she'd ever seen, and she felt a slight tinge of envy when she looked down at her own soiled clothes. She had acquired a strong fashion sense from her French grandmother, and although life in a vicarage had taught Catherine the vanity of worldliness, she didn't believe it honored God to look like a dowd. But after almost two weeks in her travel-worn gown, *dowd* was the only word to express how she felt in proximity to these exquisite creatures. After one elegant lady in a yellow ribbed-silk gown trimmed with metal lace and artificial flowers eyed her with raised brows, Catherine urged her companions to ride on. Ned and Philip, who always looked proper in their black cleric's coats with white Geneva bands at the neck and their neatly tied hair, could have little notion of how she felt.

The ride down the steep hill into town increased her discomfort as she tried to keep from leaning against Philip and at the same time craned her neck to see the unusual outcroppings of sandstone separating the fashionable houses built along the road.

At the foot of the hill they met, not a promenade of the fashionable, but a cluster of small boys and dogs chasing wildly after a runaway hoop. At first the scene amused Catherine, reminding her of similar scenes at Shoreham vicarage. But suddenly the speeding hoop veered into the roadway in front of them, and shouting boys and yapping dogs turned almost directly at Jezreel.

The startled horse skittered sharply sideways, rearing with a jerk. Catherine clutched for Philip's back, but already she had slipped beyond its grasp. With a cry, she fell to the ground.

Philip and Ned were beside her in a moment. Ned turned with a sharp command to send the boys on their way, and Philip knelt beside her. "Catherine, I'm so sorry. Are you hurt? I couldn't hold her steady. Catherine . . ."

Catherine looked at his distressed face, and a small trill of laughter broke from her. "It is a good thing you didn't hold her. By sidestepping, Jezreel managed to unload me in the only patch of long grass anywhere near this stony road. Very thoughtful of her!" And she drew one of his rare smiles which she had learned to cherish for their scarcity.

"Are you truly all right, Cath?" Ned asked.

"Truly. I wasn't the least terrified, beyond the quite natural fear of falling." She paused to consider. "I realize now that I haven't been afraid for days." With a wide smile she clasped her hands in gladness. "I am entirely recovered." And then she flung her arms out to express a relief beyond words.

Catherine had been a person of few fears. She knew a brief fear of the dark as a child, and she could still remember her father coming into her room, not hers alone, of course—one was never alone in a family of twelve—after the others were asleep. And if Father were gone, Ned would come with a simple good night, to let her know he was there and cared. Therefore, the fear hadn't lasted long.

And then there had been her one fearful experience in the woods, when at the age of twelve she had wandered too far in search of a blue jay and gotten lost. It was long after dark when she heard Ned calling, and the fear fell away as if the woods were lighted.

But her fear of horses had found no such happy ending, until today. She smiled at Philip, thinking how a fine horse was the one thing that invariably made his cool eyes glow dark and warm. And now she was free of the fear that prevented her from sharing this interest with her new friend. Just as with the help of others the small Catherine had conquered her fear of the dark and of being lost in the woods, so she had conquered her fear of horses—with the help of Philip and of God. The God, who at least in this instance, did indeed seem to be still guiding her way.

Philip remounted, and Ned gave her a leg up to her pillion seat. Then, in spite of the increased dowdiness the dark grass stains added to her dress, Catherine Perronet rode in triumph through Tunbridge Wells.

The accommodations here were unlike any others they had experienced on the journey, or were likely to on any itinerant preaching tour. The town had changed remarkably since the time of Charles I when his queen, Henrietta Maria, arrived with her court to take the spa waters and had to camp in tents on the common because so few houses or public inns had yet been built.

"Ned, are you quite sure we can afford this?" Catherine was looking at the brocade and gilt of the Louis XV furniture in the parlor, but her mind was on Philip's slim purse.

"Perhaps—," Ned began, but was interrupted by a flurry of activity as they were caught between a party arriving at the door and the landlord with the entire staff of the inn rushing to greet the new arrivals alighting from their elegant coroneted coach. At the center of the maelstrom was a tiny, sharp-featured woman, her graying brown hair tucked firmly inside a cap of the finest white linen, the severe plainness of her Spitalfields silk gown in no way hiding the excellent quality of the fabric or workmanship.

"Welcome, My Lady. My humble establishment is yours, and I your most devoted servant." The innkeeper bowed so deeply it seemed for a moment he would overbalance and fall on his nose.

The lady began giving orders for the dispatching of her entourage and possessions, all of which were carried out with the greatest alacrity. When the room had been fairly cleared of servants, trunks, and portmanteaux, the noble lady sighted the three travelers who watched from a corner of the room. "Edward Perronet. You may present yourself."

Edward stepped forward and made his bow. "Lady

Huntingdon, may I beg leave to present my sister and our companion?"

The lady inclined her head.

"Lady Huntingdon, my sister, Miss Catherine Perronet, and our friend, the Reverend Philip Ferrar."

"Ah. I recall now, Mr. Ferrar. John Wesley told me you were preaching in this area. I shall hear more of your work. You will join me for dinner." Her gaze included the three of them; then she turned to the hovering innkeeper. "You will provide accommodations for my friends on my account also." She turned back to Ned. "I dine at seven o'clock." Her exit from the room was as straightforward as a military march, the small train on her dress following in obedient folds.

The second assistant to the landlord approached the three still standing in the center of the floor. "May I show you to your rooms?"

In her room a dismayed Catherine surveyed her dress. Her only comfort was that she had washed and pressed her lawn fichu, so she would have a fresh covering around the neckline of her bodice. But what the countess would say to her soiled skirt, Catherine quailed to consider. She heated her curling iron over a candle and framed her face with small round curls, then drew the remainder of her hair into a bun on the top of her head, to be covered by her ruffled lawn cap.

It was also fortunate that when she entered the countess's private parlor with Ned and Philip at the commanded hour, the shadows in the candle-lit room concealed the most disreputable of her travel stains. And, as always, Catherine's dignified carriage overshadowed anything she wore.

The countess introduced her traveling companion, her aunt, Lady Fanny Shirley, and directed her servants to set the first course. The roast pork with turnips suited milady's taste, but the butter pond pudding would not do. "My constitution cannot abide this. Remove it at once." A servant hurried forward. "There is enough butter in that to have drowned the pig, had it been alive. I have come to the Wells to have my health restored, not further endangered by rich puddings."

The offending dish was hastily removed and replaced by jugged pigeons with pease and onions. "I more frequently take the waters at Bath," Lady Huntingdon explained to her guests, "but my condition did not respond well to my last visit there, so my physician recommended the chalybeate spring here. You must accompany me in the morning, Miss Perronet. You look entirely too peaked. You want fortifying. You know, after Dudley Lord North discovered these springs early last century, he was miraculously cured from a lingering consumptive disorder."

The other diners made appropriate responses to her monologue. Then she focused on Philip sitting on her left. "Young man, you are entirely too thin. You must eat more." She carved a thick slice of pork and placed it on his plate. "Preaching the Word of God requires stamina. You must fortify yourself physically as well as spiritually for the slings and arrows of the enemy. Have your services met with success?"

Philip responded that there had been many victories in spite of the resistance of the rabble. He was about to elaborate when the countess went on. "This is a benighted area. The season is just beginning, but already you shall see the luminaries of society on the promenade. Dr. Johnson, David Garrick, Mr. Pitt—they come here regularly now that that self-appointed potentate from Bath has undertaken to establish his routines of vice here. I speak, of course, of Beau Nash. Coffee houses, balls, concerts, gambling rooms—that is what Tunbridge Wells offers to kill the souls of those who would drink her waters for the health of their bodies."

The countess placed a pigeon and another turnip on Philip's plate. "I thank God that you have come to do battle with the evil one in his very stronghold. But it will not be easy. Not that we are ever to expect the way of our Lord to be easy, of course. But the only established church in the district is the

Chapel-of-Ease, dedicated to King Charles the Martyr, and it is little attended and is closed altogether between the seasons.

"When I was here with my chaplain, Mr. Madan, he was not allowed to preach in the Chapel-of-Ease because of his evangelical beliefs, even though, of course, he is fully ordained and a most godly man. Mount Sion, the Presbyterian place of worship, was put at his disposal; but such a man is not a dissenter and must not be forced from his own church."

All eating at the table had stopped as the countess's guests gave attention to her monologue. She paused to regard Philip. "Eat, sir. Did I not tell you to?" Philip obediently picked up his fork as the countess continued.

"Mr. Wesley also attended me here once. The Presbyterian place was freely lent for his use, but it was insufficient to contain the numbers who wished to hear. He addressed the assembled multitudes in the open air. This was a new and extraordinary occurrence at Tunbridge Wells, and it created no small stir.

"I have been forced to travel without a chaplain this time, Mr. Madan having fallen ill with an ague and Mr. Whitefield not yet recovered from his latest journey to America. But God, in His never-failing graciousness, has provided. You shall preach for me, sir."

Philip inclined his head in obedient compliance.

"Tomorrow after we take the waters, I shall inspect the subscription list at the assembly rooms to learn who is in town and draw my list. Fanny," and she turned to her aunt, "you shall send invitations to a drawing room."

"Yes, indeed, Selina," Lady Shirley replied.

"Sir Thomas I'Anson shall open his home for me again as he did when last Mr. Madan preached here."

"Yes, indeed, Selina."

The servants entered to remove the dishes. "Nothing sweet," the countess directed. "You may set a cheddar cheese and some nuts, and perhaps dried apricots if they're nice."

"Yes, Milady, very nice indeed."

She looked at Philip. "And a dish of sweet whey for this young man and the other young people. But no nutmeg. My physician warns me it is most harmful to the constitution."

Catherine quickly raised her napkin to her mouth to cover a smile. They obediently ate the milk junket with sugar and cream, flavored with rosewater but no nutmeg.

Later when the party was sitting at ease around the room sipping cups of finest Hyson tea, taken with milk to lessen its stimulating effect, Catherine confided to Lady Fanny Shirley, "My portmanteau was lost in a flood. I fear I have nothing appropriate even for drinking the waters in polite company, let alone attending a drawing room in the home of Sir Thomas I'Anson."

"The waters are drunk in dishabille. Have you no morning robe?" Lady Shirley asked in her soft voice.

Catherine wanted to laugh, but she was afraid the countess would frown on such levity in her parlor where she now engaged Ned and Philip in theological conversation on her strictly-held Calvinist tenets. "Alas, no closer than Greenwich," Catherine said. "One's needs are quite simple on a preaching circuit."

"Yes, I can guess they might be. You are to be commended for your courage in making such a journey. Although I am aware many women do so, I know I should never attempt it. Why, I've heard that Mrs. Murray even attended Mr. Wesley into Ireland." Lady Shirley emphasized her words with a small shudder. "But as to your wardrobe, I fancy we can contrive something. You are much taller than I, but perhaps we could let down a petticoat and gather up the overskirt into puffs in the shepherdess style. It was quite the rage when last we were in London and would look very charming on you—if Selina approves," she added hastily.

Selina approved. So the next day Catherine appeared on the Pantiles in a charming sprigged muslin dress worn shepherdess-style over a fashionably short petticoat. Lady Fanny Shirley had even been able to produce new blue ribbons for Catherine's wide straw hat. Fanny had at first suggested pink, but

Catherine did not feel that was the most flattering color for her dark complexion, and so was delighted with the light blue.

Catherine and her escorts entered the colonnaded row of shops shaded by lime trees along one side of the promenade—the heart of Tunbridge Wells. There a large crowd of the fashionable gathered every morning around the chalybeate spring at the entrance to the square. And, indeed, they were in dishabille, as Lady Fanny had predicted. The men wore long damask dressing gowns which swept the paving tiles, or the shorter banyon, cut similar to a dress coat with flared skirts, but with the hem ending well below the knees. All the men were wigless, covering their shaved heads either with caps of fabric matching their dressing gowns or with the more fashionable turbans. The women wore simple muslin saques, most of them with long, elegantly embroidered white muslin aprons.

A small group of musicians entertained the visitors as they waited for the dipper to ladle their glass of water from her sunken stall beneath the colonnade. The dipper's appointment, by legal act, was the gift of the Lord of Rusthall Manor, owner of the area. The small sum Edward paid her for their glasses was not for the water but for her service.

Catherine took the glass from her brother and sipped the slightly yellow liquid. "Fah, it tastes like rust."

"Iron water," Ned agreed. "From the forge of St. Dunstan."

Catherine returned her glass to the dipper. "What are you talking about, Ned?" She placed her hand lightly on her brother's arm and smiled at Philip on the other side of her as they strolled up the shaded promenade.

"It's the source of the amazing properties of the water," Ned replied. "In the tenth century, St. Dunstan had a forge nearby. He was visited there one day by a most seductive young lady whom the saint immediately recognized as the devil. The holy man seized a pair of tongs from the fire and gripped the devil by the nose. Whereupon the devil plunged his face into the cooling waters of the spring, thereby imparting to them forever their distinctive metallic tang."

Catherine smiled at her brother's story and then looked up at Philip, catching one of his brief smiles—which sometimes made her want to cry.

They went up the steps onto the Upper Walk and strolled past houses and shops fronted by rows of Italianate columns, past a general store, the Musick Gallery, the Assembly Rooms where later in the day Beau Nash would preside over the gaming tables, coffee houses filled with patrons bearing the latest gossip, and booksellers, where already a few who had taken their water early were gathering to pen letters or the "water poetry" so popular in the town.

At the end of the walk they turned and left the colonnade for the more open promenade under the lime trees, walking on the flat paving tiles that gave the area its name. They had almost returned the length of the Pantiles to the dipper's stall when a short rotund man in a full-bottomed wig and embroidered red damask coat puffed up the avenue toward them.

"Sirs and Madam," he punctuated each word by tapping on the tiles with his walking stick, "I have the honor of being Squire Penshurst."

Apparently their polite replies to this information did not fulfill his expectations. "Of Penshurst Hall," he added with an additional tap. "I am the local magistrate."

As Catherine wondered if they were to congratulate him upon this achievement, he drew from his pocket a large piece of parchment with an official seal attached to it. "It has come to my attention that you have held irregular preaching services in this vicinity, and as the duly sworn representative of His Majesty's law, it is my duty to inform you that we shall permit no such activities in Tunbridge Wells."

"Sir, it is–" Ned began, but got no further as a small figure in a large white cap took command.

"Good morning, Squire Penshurst. I see you have met my

friends Mr. and Miss Perronet and Mr. Ferrar. I shall present them at a drawing room I am holding at Sir Thomas I'Anson's home tomorrow night." The round figure in the cherry coat put the warrant back into his pocket and bobbed a bow of assent to Her Ladyship. "I shall expect to see you there, Squire."

And, indeed, Squire Penshurst was among the elegant assembly that filled the drawing room in Sir I'Anson's Palladian home atop fashionable Mount Ephraim. The Countess of Huntingdon presided as hostess and made the introductions. "Lady Lincoln and Baroness Banks, may I present our speaker for the evening, the Reverend Philip Ferrar."

The baroness extended her hand. "How do you do? Are you connected to the Yorkshire Ferrars, sir?"

Philip bowed over the white hand. "I am from London, My Lady."

Observing from across the room, Catherine gave a grateful thought to the orphanage matron's careful drilling in manners that could teach a foundling to be at ease in this exalted company.

". . . the Duchess of Richmond . . ." The countess continued her tour of introduction around the room and then took a seat in the center as Sir Thomas's liveried servants handed round refreshments.

"Mr. Loggan." She signaled a powdered gentleman in a suit of Genoa velvet with a gold-tissue brocaded waistcoat to take the seat beside her. "I viewed your paintings in London."

"Indeed, I am honored, My Lady."

"Charming. Quite charming. You have an excellent eye. But you must avoid an overuse of too bold colors. You will get nowhere by shocking refined tastes."

"I thank you for your condescension in noticing me, My Lady."

"It is well that you came tonight. You did not attend when Mr. Madan spoke."

"Indeed, My Lady, I was not in Tunbridge Wells at the time."

"Very careless of you, Loggan. You must take more care for your soul. Mr. Madan exhorted all to seek the Lord while He may be found. Whilst Mr. Madan was offering that gracious invitation of our Lord, 'Come unto Me, all ye that are labor and are heavy laden,' a man in the congregation dropped down and instantly expired."

Mr. Loggan shook out the lace frill at his wrist. "Egad, that must have caused a sensation."

"Indeed, so strong and general an influence on a congregation I seldom remember seeing. Many were melted to tears and seemed resolved to fly from the wrath to come."

"Very understandable."

The company having finished their refreshments, the countess called for the general attention of her guests and introduced Edward and Catherine who were to present a number by the greatest hymn-writer of their day, Mr. Charles Wesley. With her usual grave solemnity Catherine took her seat at the harpsichord and after a few sharp, clear chords, blended her voice with her brother's: "Love divine, all loves excelling, / Joy of heav'n to earth come down; . . . Jesus, Thou art all compassion, / Pure, unbounded love Thou art; / Visit us with Thy salvation, / Enter ev'ry trembling heart."

At the conclusion of the song the countess introduced Philip, and Catherine sent him a small smile of encouragement, knowing this audience could be far more daunting than any fireworks-throwing or bull-baiting rabble. Philip stood at the end of the room, his silver-blond hair and white bands glowing like lights at the top of his tall, black-clad figure. With perfect self-possession he spoke to the distinguished assemblage on the text, "The fear of the Lord is the beginning of wisdom." And every word rang absolutely true because spoken by a man whose relationship with Christ was more than head knowledge. He had true fear of the Lord based on reverential awe of His love and greatness.

Catherine watched as Philip spoke in the elegant drawing

room, and she admired how he was carrying everything off. Whatever inward struggles he experienced, he was neither awkward nor exuberant. He brought to the situation the same quiet detachment he had shown in all other occasions; and now, with the full glare of the most elegant nobility turned upon him, his solemn grace was as perfect as any to the manor born. Amazing in one who had been essentially on his own since childhood. God had given this man a natural excellence that needed no other guidance than His grace.

At the end of the sermon many appeared genuinely moved. It seemed truly that "Those who came to scoff, remained to pray," as Wesley had reported of a similar meeting. "I am moved to consider what you say." The artist Loggan shook Philip's hand. "I would hear more of this."

The countess was delighted. When the last guest had departed, she turned to her speaker and musicians. "A remarkable service. Many were cut to the heart. Truly God was in our midst to wound and to heal. Such happy indications of God's approval induce me to hope that He will smile on my humble efforts. I mean to take up the sword for the glory of His great name and the good of the people of this place. Today has given me assurance that He will ultimately crown my efforts with distinguished and lasting success."

She walked the length of the room with her rapid steps and then sat on a straight chair, her back ramrod, her small, pointed chin forward. "Perhaps I shall build a residence here on Mount Ephraim that I might work more among these people. But I am forever conscious that every effort is impotent without God's almighty aid. I cry continually to Him for wisdom and strength. What am I, that He should condescend to make me instrumental in communicating any good to others? Is it not a sobering thought? I am humbled in the dust before Him. It is the Lord, *the Lord Himself* that has done the work. The treasure is in an earthen vessel, but the excellency of the power is of God *only*."

She sat for a moment with her head bowed. Then suddenly

the head jerked up, and the dark, bright eyes snapped. "Miss Perronet, I do not like you riding pillion across the countryside. It isn't ladylike. I understand the gentlemen must go on tomorrow, but you will remain here with me, and I shall return you to London at the end of the month."

"Your Ladyship, I thank you for your concern. But my father expects me. I cannot disappoint him."

The countess blinked as if she could not take in disagreement with her plans. Her thin cheeks became even thinner, and for a moment Catherine feared her response. Then the countess spoke. "Fine man, your father. Perhaps the most heavenly minded man I know. Give him my regards."

*T*he next morning Catherine hoped that her bold behavior had not placed her in the countess's bad graces, but the ride through the glorious May morning assured her she had made the right decision. The road led between ferns carpeting the incline on both sides of the path and across little streams meandering through spinneys of white-barked birches. Birds sang from hedgerows laced with blossoms. Masses of purple and yellow wildflowers colored the fields, and wild daisies smaller than farthings grew from the shortest of stems.

"Philip, pray stop a moment. I should like to collect some samples for my wildflower book."

He pulled Jezreel to a halt and helped Catherine dismount. "You don't have this variety in your collection?"

"Not this particular shade of lavender." Her long fingers spread the leaves aside and pinched the stems to gather a small nosegay. "One of the things I most look forward to in being at Shoreham again is walking in my dear woods."

As they rode further into Catherine's native corner of Kent, she recognized a growing tranquility and felt a new contentment in being with Philip. They could ride for miles with only the briefest of comments on the scenery. Then quite suddenly one of them would begin a conversation, and they would talk without pause for an equal number of miles. Either way, Catherine found a repose she had never known in the companionship of another. And one of the chief gratifications was her certainty that Philip, who had such need of fellowship, found equal tranquility in her company.

And whether they were discussing a deep spiritual truth, the meaning of a poem she had read lately, or merely a commonplace observation, Catherine felt she had never been listened to so totally. Philip's capacity for giving his absolute attention was one of his most endearing charms. Even though she sat behind him, obliged to talk to the back of his head, there would come the little nod that told her he was listening. And for all his customary silence, his mind was extraordinarily active. Whenever he made a comment, it was incisive and to the point but always spoken with a characteristic gentleness.

With the hours passing so pleasantly, it seemed impossible that evening shadows should already be lengthening, but then the pathway through thick woods curved sharply, and Catherine knew they were nearly home. "Whenever I'm away, this is how I think of Shoreham—buried under the trees, so green and protected." Another curve in the path, and she saw ahead of her the dearly loved golden stone vicarage with its high curving wall around the large garden where Charity Perronet managed to keep flowers blooming from spring to autumn.

The many wings and gables of the house showed where it had been built onto through the centuries—first the low, gray rock two-room structure; then a red brick wing added at the same time the square Norman tower was put on the church; and now the lovely golden Georgian wing with the curving fanlight over the door. A symphony of familiar sounds sang Catherine's welcome home—birds twittering in the lime trees, chickens clucking from the henhouse, laughter from the inn around the corner, and the voices of children in the vicarage yard.

Then sixteen-year-old John saw the travelers approach. He

gave a shout that brought family and servants running to meet them. It was Catherine's first visit home since she had left to work for the Society in London, and now she wondered how she had managed to stay away so long. Her mother, wisps of graying hair escaping from her cap, engulfed them each in her comfortable embrace and warm smile. Vincent, his full-bottomed wig slightly askew, greeted them more quietly but no less warmly, his pleasure shining from his kindly eyes. And Damaris, Henry, William, Philothea, Thomas, and John all gathered around to welcome them.

"Betsy, we shall be three more at dinner. Come in, my dears. You know your rooms. Philip, Ned will show you. I'm sure you'll want to wash. Philly, you and Tom take cans of hot water up for them." Charity Perronet managed to direct the entire household without ever raising her voice.

All was orderly bustle when they gathered again in the dining room a short time later. Catherine noted Philip's pause at the door; he hung back as if not sure of his place. Only the slightest tightening of his straight mouth showed his nervousness; but as he stood aloof, Catherine could see him as he must have been at the orphanage, watching the others, but never fully part of them. Such a contrast to her own family, with a dozen noisy siblings all belonging to each other. Their eyes met, and Catherine smiled to let him know she welcomed him as part of the family.

When they had all found a place at the table, Vincent stood and offered grace, remembering the needs of the parish, mentioning each one of his children by name, and including Philip as well. By the time he concluded with a doxology the roast joint in front of him had cooled considerably, but not the diners' appetites.

Vincent carved the roast while Charity served the potted venison. Dishes of currant suet pudding and boiled parsnips with carrots were passed.

"Well, Damaris, are you still the mainstay of the Shoreham

Methodists?" Edward asked his maiden sister, who had elected to live at home and take charge of the Society work there.

"It continues to grow remarkably, Ned. We hold preaching in Father's kitchen every Friday night, but we shall soon outgrow even that room."

"One of Damaris's special tasks is seeing to the care of itinerant preachers when they are in the area; so if you find any lack in the hospitality, Philip, you must apply to her." The gentle Vincent spoke in a teasing manner, but his pride in his daughter's work showed in his eyes.

"Quite right for the daughter of the man who is often called the Archbishop of Methodism, Father," Ned said.

"And what of your preaching tour, Son? Have you met much resistance?"

Edward recounted some of their hardships at the hands of the rabble. Vincent shook his head. "So much of that could be avoided if only our preachers were allowed to use the church buildings."

Edward suddenly struck the table as if he had just come to a hard decision. "As we are all family here, I shall speak my mind boldly on a matter to which I have given considerable thought." An unusual cutting edge to his voice made Catherine hold her breath. She had noted his sometimes brooding quiet on the trip and knew that, although he was the kindest of brothers to her, he was capable of being hotheaded and sharp-tongued.

"We must give thought to separation."

"Edward!" Charity's voice was the first to break the shocked silence. "And your father a vicar of the Church of England these past thirty years, twenty-one of them right here in this very church. And you and your brother Charl ordained priests! How can you say such a thing?"

"I am sorry, Mother. But I believe we will come to it. Our brother Charl means to bring it up at the next conference. We should grant license to our own ministers to serve the sacraments."

"You are thinking of becoming a nonjuror, Son?" Vincent asked in his quiet voice.

"I don't know, Father. I can see that I spoke in haste, especially in front of my younger brothers and sister, but the problem is serious, indeed. Philip here is one of the finest men I've ever heard preach; must he spend his life in a cow pasture? He was dismissed from his curacy for enthusiasm and has been without a post these two years, although he has made frequent application. Something must be done. A dissenting chapel must be better than no place at all!" In spite of himself, his voice rose to an impassioned pitch.

"I would remind you, Son, that our Lord had nowhere to lay His sacred head. And His Sermon on the Mount was a pretty remarkable precedent of field preaching. When John Wesley was last here, he told me of the huge multitude he preached to in Moorfields. For usefulness, there is none comparable to field preaching, he said. What building except St. Paul's Church could contain such a large congregation as a field? One can command thrice the number in the open air. And do you not feel the convicting, convincing power of God at work among the people in the fields?"

Edward agreed that was true.

"Then, my Son, do not despise the means which our Lord hath put at your hand. I believe one hindrance of the work of God in York has been the neglect of field preaching; and I am apt to think that many of the hearers at your meetings have scarcely ever heard a Methodist before, or perhaps any other preacher. What but field preaching could reach these poor sinners? Are not their souls also precious in the sight of God?"

"Your reasoned words are a help to me. I shall attempt to control my impatience, Father. But I confess to feeling a shadow of bitterness over the situation at times."

"Oh, no, no, my Son. Pray earnestly for the grubbing out of all roots of bitterness. You must replace them with love. Love is all."

There was a knock at the door, and Betsy hurried from the kitchen to answer it. "It's Mr. Claygate, sir. Come for the Bible reading. I 'ad 'im sit in the parlor."

"You still hold your nightly Bible readings, Father?" Catherine asked.

"Indeed, Daughter. But I have put the hour back to seven. And a good thing too, or we should have missed this stimulating conversation tonight. Never fear to speak to your family of what concerns your heart, my children." Vincent rose. "Now, let us go to prayers."

The large vicarage parlor was crowded as family, servants, and parishioners gathered for nightly Bible reading and prayers. And Catherine was sure that, in spite of all that had been said in favor of field preaching, one of the prayers Philip would offer would still be for the Lord to open the way to a parish of his own. She too prayed that that petition would be granted.

The next morning being Sunday, the village bell-ringers put to full use the eight bells in the Shoreham parish church of St. Peter and St. Paul. Catherine entered with the other villagers through the porch, which had been built in the fifteenth century from the root of a huge upended oak. She took her seat on the second pew where she had worshiped since she was three years old.

As she sang the familiar hymns, listened to the lessons, and knelt for prayers with these people she had grown up among, the conflicts and struggles of the past weeks seemed to slip away. It seemed impossible that there could be such disturbances in God's world. The collect for that fifth Sunday after Easter seemed to hold the key to all problems:

> O Lord, from whom all good things do come; Grant to us
> thy humble servants, that by Thy holy inspiration, we may
> think those things that be good, and by Thy merciful guiding
> may perform the same; through our Lord Jesus Christ, amen.

While her father preached, she let her eyes wander over the dear church. She had always loved the dark wood-vaulted ceiling. One of her earliest memories was of peeking up at it when her eyes should have been closed in prayer, counting the golden stars embedded in the wood. One time Ned caught her at her game and reprimanded her later—the stars weren't there to be counted; they were to serve as reminders of the infinity of God, and counting them would spoil everything.

She disagreed, however. One warm Saturday afternoon when the church was empty, she slipped into its lovely, cool stone interior, lay right down on the flagged floor, and began counting. But she kept getting confused and having to start all over again. In the end she fell asleep and received a dreadful scolding for not helping Elizabeth peel the potatoes for supper.

Later that afternoon she recounted the memory to Philip. "I am surprised to hear of the scolding. It seems to me that your family never raises their voices to one another."

"Well, perhaps we only do so in a very restrained way. And then we always say we are sorry as soon as the moment has passed."

They crossed the vicarage garden back to the church. Catherine had volunteered to take the children's service for her father if Philip would help her, which he readily agreed to do. She turned to him now against the backdrop of the rambling vicarage and its riotous garden, with their talk of her happy, loving family hanging in the air. She saw him standing there, tall and thin in his dark suit, and thought how austere his life had been.

When she looked at him a short time later as he explained the story of the Good Samaritan to the village children, she saw his face aglow as it was only when he preached. A great wave of feeling washed over her; it was a feeling she couldn't identify but that she wanted to clasp to her, in spite of the ache it brought with it.

It was to be a day of strange feelings for Catherine. When her family gathered around the parlor fireplace after Evensong,

Philip was the last to enter. Again he paused just outside the doorway, and she saw him alone, as she was accustomed to thinking of him. Then he entered and sat down and was suddenly part of the family when young Thomas climbed on his lap and Philothea sat so close as to be leaning on him. It was as if in this rural vicarage Philip Ferrar had dropped into place.

When they had their fill of visiting and cold meats, the family slowly straggled off to bed. Vincent and Charity were the last to leave them. "Thank you for giving us that fine sermon at Evensong. You can come preach for me anytime," Vincent said to Philip. Then he kissed his daughter good night.

Charity also kissed Catherine. "We shall begin our parish visits at nine o'clock in the morning. Old Mrs. Claygate is very poorly, and the Ightham children weren't at the children's service today, and—oh, well, there are so many. My dear, it will be so good to have you visiting with me."

Then Philip and Catherine had the fireside all to themselves. For the moment it seemed as if this parish where they were preaching, teaching, and visiting the sick and needy was their own, as Midhurst must have been for Philip. Catherine poured out a final cup of tea for her companion who sat with his feet up on the hob. The very "everydayness" of it made her feel as if she were a little girl playing house. But she longed for the reality.

It seemed to Catherine that this return to her home brought constant revelations and understandings as she accompanied her mother the next morning. She watched as Charity dealt with the needs of the people of the parish. Gradually, it was as if she were watching a new person—or perhaps, for the first time, a real person in the place of the generalized, comfortable image of "mother." She had always seen her mother as an extension of her father, a woman who found her being in her many children as she directed the household to revolve around

Vincent. Father's meals were always on time, composed of his favorite foods, prepared the way he liked them; Father's study hours were always to be undisturbed by children, parishioners, or other clergymen; Father's work must receive her help—visiting the sick, distributing charity from the poor box, arranging flowers on the altar; and Father's children must always be orderly, clean, well-behaved, respectful. Not that Vincent Perronet was a demanding tyrant—a kinder, softer-spoken soul couldn't be imagined. But this was the natural order of things.

It had given Catherine's childhood a focus, a pattern, a security. Father was the center of the household and the parish, just as John Wesley was the center of the Methodist Society, the King was the center of England, and God was the center of the universe. But now Catherine realized how important a focus her mother was for her own sake—the love and warmth and comfort she shared unstintingly with her twelve children and the three hundred souls in their parish.

Charity Perronet was far more than an extension of her husband; she was a person who chose to be a helpmeet and to fulfill Christ's call to servanthood. And for the first time in her life, Catherine truly saw her mother—an insight a bit like the first time an infant sees the world outside. And with it came a new love and appreciation for her mother.

But most important, she felt a desire to carry on in her mother's tradition of love and service. She would be the person God created her to be, serving out of love—if only God would show her how and where. "O God," she prayed, "surely You would not have given me this desire if You did not have a place for me to use it."

The final stop for mother and daughter was in the center of the village where the Misses Simpson plied their expert needles in the little Tudor shop that was also their home. With her mother's help and the fluttery attendance of the elder Miss Simpson, Catherine looked through the pattern cards and fabrics and chose an open gown to be made from dimity of simple texture but lively pattern, with little bouquets of scattered flowers. The flowers, stomacher, and petticoat reflected Catherine's love of nature as she selected a clear blue like the sky and the bluebells that grew in the woods around Shoreham in the spring.

"You have chosen well, my dear," Charity told her. "Buying good fabric is never extravagant because it lasts so much longer. Sometimes I buy French fabric, but only from established shops—one must be careful not to support the runners by buying smuggled products. This lace will make a lovely trimming for the neckline and sleeve flounces."

Catherine hesitated. The lace her mother held was lovely, but many Society members avoided such worldliness. She had never considered removing it from the dresses she already owned, but wondered about the propriety of ordering it on a new gown.

"There can be nothing displeasing to God in a bit of lace, my dear. Even your father's best surplice has a trim of lace on it." Charity handed the lace to the dressmaker at Catherine's nod. "And now we must hurry home for tea. I told Betsy to make a special treat."

But even the veiled hint from her mother and the broad smiles from her siblings did nothing to prod Catherine's suspicions—not until she had been served a thick slice of seed cake with a dish of sweet tea. Philothea burst out between giggles, "She's forgotten, hasn't she? Cath, don't you truly know what day this is?"

Catherine looked puzzled. "No, I've given it no thought. I lost all account of the days on our travels. It must be May . . . oh, is it truly the twelfth of May? My birthday?"

She had to set her tea dish aside very quickly before she was engulfed in congratulatory hugs and birthday kisses.

"And you too, Philip, you must wish Cath happiness." Philly led their guest forward.

"Felicitations, Catherine."

A GENTLE CALLING

"Oh, fah! It won't do if you don't kiss her. Don't be so shy, Philip." Philothea gave him a sisterly shove that almost landed his lanky form in Catherine's lap.

He bent over gravely, picked up her hand, and brushed it with his lips. "Many happy returns." And suddenly Catherine felt they would be.

Ten-year-old Philothea applauded the performance of the guest she had adopted wholeheartedly as her personal property. "Well done! And when is your birthday, Philip?"

He withdrew to the back of the company. "I fear I have no idea. I have never given the subject any thought."

Catherine chilled with fear for his feelings. She knew how sensitive he was about his foundling status. But she could think of nothing to distract her little sister as Philly insisted, "Oh, but you must know how old you are."

"Yes, I know that. I've had the good fortune to accomplish thirty years."

"How odd not to know your birthday." Philothea frowned at the problem. "Perhaps you could celebrate your saint's day. May first is Saint Philip and Saint James's Day—pity Philip didn't get one of his own; the other apostles did. I suppose it was because he was so quiet. If he'd talked more, he'd have more stories in the Bible, and then they'd have given him his own day." She thought for a moment. "But don't feel bad. I'm sure he was really a very important apostle. The collect says, 'Following the steps of Thy holy apostles, Saint Philip and Saint James, we may steadfastly walk in the way that leadeth to eternal life.' Pity it's just past. Will you mind dreadfully waiting a whole year for your birthday?"

Philip started to say that he wouldn't mind in the least, but Damaris joined in with another suggestion. "Perhaps you could celebrate your spiritual birthday."

"Oh, yes! A splendid idea," exclaimed Philly. "The day you were born again. That *would* be a birthday. Do you remember when it was, Philip?"

99

"Yes, it was the second Sunday in Trinity. I remember because Trinity term had just begun when I had the opportunity of calling on William Law."

Catherine steered the conversation away from the uncomfortable subject of birthdays. "How fortunate you were—to be able to counsel with a man who has influenced so many."

"Yes, I was perhaps the one man in all Cambridge who prayed in a formal way every day; but Law made me see that saying the right words with the mouth while the heart is far from God is worthless in God's sight."

"And you found assurance of salvation then?" Vincent asked.

"Truly. As soon as I saw that my hope and trust must be fixed solely in my Creator and Redeemer. Law showed me that attempting to appease or please God by an outward system of good works was totally erroneous. When I saw that all I needed to do was open my heart and receive from Christ His righteousness, I knew a great peace."

"Eight Sundays after Easter," announced Philothea who had been looking up Trinity Sunday in the "Table of Lessons" in the Prayer Book. "So the second Sunday in Trinity is nine weeks after Easter, which will be—," she paused to count on her fingers, "the second Sunday in June. You must remember to celebrate."

He nodded solemnly at the child's earnest instruction.

"Might I have another piece of cake, Mother?" John held out an empty plate.

"Here, have mine." Philip's response was so natural, and he placed the cake on the younger boy's plate so quickly that it was a moment before Catherine realized what had happened. Back in a group, Philip had reacted as he undoubtedly had at the orphanage to the needs of another. She wondered how often his unselfishness had led him to give his food away?

"And now in honor of this day, dear Sister," Edward bowed to Catherine, "I have the pleasure of announcing that I have completed my new hymn."

"Oh, Ned, how splendid! Is it the one you were working on during our trip?"

"Yes, I have seldom had a composition cost me so much effort, but I flatter myself that I have captured some of the stateliness I sought." He began to read.

> All hail the power of Jesus' name!
> Let angels prostrate fall;
> Bring forth the royal diadem,
> And crown Him Lord of all!

Catherine felt a thrill as her mind's eye glimpsed the splendor of that heavenly throne where her King and Lord ruled the universe. Each of the four verses brought smiles and nods from the appreciative audience until at last Edward concluded with:

> O that with yonder sacred throng
> We at His feet may fall!
> We'll join the everlasting song,
> And crown Him Lord of all!

"Oh, Ned!" Catherine was the first to respond. "It's wonderful! So worshipful and majestic! I can feel the greatness of God. It makes me want to shout glory to Him."

"Catherine, I couldn't imagine you so demonstrative." Edward laughed.

"Well, my spirit shouts even if I don't," she amended.

Charity dabbed at her eyes with a linen handkerchief, but whatever she was about to say was interrupted by a knock at the door.

Vincent moved to answer it before any of the servants could respond. "Why, Charl, what an unexpected pleasure!"

He stepped back to admit his newly arrived son, but his smile faded as he looked at the messenger's face.

"Ned, I am sent for you. Your wife is dangerously ill."

*T*hey set out at first light, and by continually pressing their horses and themselves, the riders covered the eighteen miles from Shoreham to Greenwich in just five hours. Edward rode always at the front, urging his horse and his companions to greater speed, showing by the sharpness of his voice how near to distraction he was. At Kidbrooke, a mile from Greenwich, he kicked his horse and galloped ahead.

"Go with him, Charl," Catherine told her brother. "I shall be there soon, and he may need your support."

When she and Philip arrived half an hour later, the stable-boy was still cooling the two horses. Joseph helped Catherine dismount, but Philip stayed in the saddle. "Shall I see you in, or would it be best that I not intrude?"

"Oh, please come in." The thought of his riding off was suddenly more than she could bear. She looked toward the doctor's black carriage waiting by the house. "I don't know what we may find inside. I should be grateful for your support."

And having him beside her did make walking into the unknown easier. The house was ominously quiet. Catherine paused at the foot of the stairs.

"Ned is upstairs." Charl's voice from the parlor startled her.

"Is—is she—"

"Alive. But very weak. She lost much blood."

"The babe?"

Charl shook his head, and Catherine nodded in reply; she had feared it would be so.

"Thank God, Durial's alive. I dreaded the worst." She turned to Philip. "I must go up to her."

He nodded.

Audrey, hovering outside her mistress's door in case she should be wanted, ushered Catherine into the dimly lit room. The physician, thoroughly in charge, was addressing Durial. "You've had a very narrow escape, and you are not to stir from that bed for a fortnight. Do I make myself clear? I shall instruct your cook in making a restorative elixir from the juice of red meat, to be taken morning and night without fail. And I shall call again in the morning."

"Is he just now come?" Catherine whispered to her sister Elizabeth.

"No, no. He sat with her all night and then came back this afternoon. We despaired of her life."

"What happened?"

"She fell. It was the spring cleaning, and she *would* take a hand in turning out the linen closets." Elizabeth moved to the door to see the doctor out, leaving Ned and Catherine alone with the patient.

"Durial, dear, we are so sorry." Catherine moved closer to the bed and received a weak smile from her sister-in-law. Even in the dim room, Durial's pallor was frightful. She was whiter than her linen sheets and seemed shrunken into her pillows. "My husband, I am so sorry. If only I hadn't been so headstrong and house-proud. Now I'll never have aught to give you but a clean house."

Ned moved to take her hand in both of his. "No, no, my dear. There shall be others."

Durial moved her head from side to side slowly, as if the

movement cost her great effort. "No, Dr. Eltham says there shall be no more."

Edward turned his head so that his wife couldn't see the pain, but Catherine saw. After a moment he turned back. "But I shall have your precious self, Durial. Now rest and fret not."

Durial relaxed at his words and closed her eyes. "I shall sit with her," Ned said. "You get some rest, Catherine."

Catherine was still wearing her mud-stained traveling cloak and half-boots. She went to her room and washed before returning downstairs. The parlor seemed unaccountably chill and empty. "Where's Philip?" she asked Charl.

"I tried to persuade him to sup with us, but he seemed to think his presence would be an intrusion."

The room no longer seemed merely empty to her—it was desolate.

The room Philip entered was equally desolate. For the first time, he saw it in its emptiness and shabbiness. Its bleakness brought to mind winter evenings when Matron would send her charges out to take the air after classes. The other children would join in rolling hoops or a noisy game of tutball. But Philip preferred to stay to himself, breaking up the ice from the puddles on the north side of the building with a stick. What began as a simple time-filler became something of a challenge, and he worked hard to keep ahead of the refreezing.

But he had never learned how to chip at the emotional ice inside. Keeping to himself had always seemed such a good answer to his fear of abandonment—if there was no one else in his life, if his relationship to God was the only one he relied on, there could be no one to leave him. But these past weeks with the Perronets—with Catherine especially—had produced a hairline crack in the ice. He now wondered whether the infraction should be encouraged.

In not letting others get to know the man inside, he had not gotten very well acquainted with himself—with that emotional, feeling part he had always kept so tightly controlled. Could he be more truly open to God if he were to be more open to those around him? He shivered at the thought of becoming transparent and vulnerable, of being hurt once more, as he had been at Midhurst and then over Sally Gwynne.

Philip encouraged the uncooperative flame in his fireplace, ate the soup and brown bread Mrs. Watson provided, and turned to his bed, just as he had turned to his iron cot at the orphan asylum. It had been the last in the row, and he had found that lying with his back to the room was as good as being alone. But now there was no need for that device to achieve solitude.

The next morning Philip went to the Foundery custom-house to inquire of William Briggs, John Wesley's secretary, if there was any mail for him or further itinerary assignments. He was surprised to find Elizabeth Perronet also in the office. "I have taken to helping Mr. Briggs with some of his correspondence when I can be spared at home," she explained with a hint of a blush.

"And how is Mrs. Edward Perronet this morning?"

"Her sleep was much disturbed. Dr. Eltham was there when I left. But Ned insisted I should come assist here while Catherine teaches her class. Ned won't leave Durial. I fear he blames himself much for being away when the accident occurred."

"It is said by many that itinerant preachers should not be wed." Philip nodded.

"Here is a letter come for you last week." Briggs handed the wax-sealed paper to Philip. "And you will preach the evening service tonight?"

"I'll be happy to. Thank you, William. I hope to hear of your sister-in-law's speedy recovery, Miss Perronet." Philip took his leave.

In the courtyard he perused his letter. It was from his old friend George Whitefield.

The 9 of 4, Glous.

My dear Philip,

As I wish to inform my friends at the Foundery of my recent return from America and report on my work there, but am not assured of my welcome in the Society, nor of my desire to be so, I shall communicate with one whom I have always known to be unfailing in his generosity and fair in his judgment, that he might advise me. I have heard the most disturbing reports while abroad. Can it be that John Wesley preaches universal redemption? That cannot be consistent with the scriptural doctrine of election. Can Wesley have strayed so far?

Although my heart aches at hearing that the work may have fallen astray (although I am assured that that most excellent lady, the Countess of Huntingdon, continues faithful in the doctrines of Calvin), the work in America progresses apace. I had great success in Philadelphia in raising money for my school and orphanage in Georgia, which I feel is the heart of my work. I employed that most excellent American, Benjamin Franklin, as a printer, who after my sermon confessed he had been determined to give nothing, since I refused to locate the orphan house at Philadelphia. But upon hearing me preach, he said he began to soften and concluded to give copper. "Another stroke decided me to give silver," he said. And at the finish he emptied his pocket into the collector's dish, gold and all. I should most heartily like to build a school for negroes in Philadelphia.

Dr. Franklin said it was wonderful to see the change soon made in the manners of their inhabitants after my revival services. I met only one case of rudeness—and that from a non-Episcopal divine. "I am sorry to see you here," he said.

"So is the devil," I replied.

And the Lord continues faithful in that part of the country which they call New England, where my friend Jonathan Edwards is one of the few truly awakened preachers. I am persuaded that there, as in England, the generality of preachers talk of an unknown and unfelt Christ. The reason why congregations have been dead is because they have dead men preaching to them. How can dead men beget living children?

And I thank God, the Harvard Awakening continues, where, to the consternation of much of its faculty, I preached against the liberalism making its way into that formerly excellent institution for ordinands. I was told subsequently that the students now are full of God.

Advise me how I shall go on, as regards our friends, and I shall remain,

Yr ever affect,
George Whitefield

His mind on how he might advise his friend and try to heal the rift between these strong leaders of the Methodist movement, Philip went on into the Foundery and back to the book room where the newly arrived printing of Charles Wesley's hymns was causing much interest. Then he realized, to his consternation, he was simply wandering around without purpose, and he took himself to his room to prepare for the evening service.

Several hundred ardent voices sang at the leading of a Society worker who opened the service that evening. Philip sang the words of the song with his mouth, but his heart missed his musical companions of the circuit trip.

In his sermon he spoke of the great, loving heart of Christ, so open to all who would come, so ready to receive sinful men. No sins were too great to be forgiven, no person too lost to be found by Him. And at the close of the service, it was apparent that Christ was ready also to receive sinful women, as a wretched-looking female waited at the back of the chapel to speak to Philip.

"You would have words with me, Sister?" He hoped to make his voice kind to calm the fear in her eyes.

She pushed a scraggle of red hair into her cap with a roughened hand. "Ah, sir. I was accidentally passing the door, and 'ear-ing the voice of someone preaching, I did what I 'ave never been in the 'abit of doing. I come in."

"You were right to do so. You are most welcome."

"I 'eard you say that Jesus Christ was so willing to receive sinners that 'e made no objection to receiving the devil's castaways. Now, sir, I am cast down so low that I was returning from seeking work in a bagnio when I passed your door."

"You had gone to sell yourself?"

"That was my attempt. I cannot keep food in my children's mouths. I thought this a way to provide for them, but they wouldn't 'ave me. To be turned away from a brothel is in truth to be one of the devil's castaways. Do you think, sir, that Jesus Christ would receive me?"

"There isn't the least doubt of it," Philip assured her, and he called two of the Society women to join him in praying for her.

When her radiant face gave assurance of new life inside, Philip asked where she lived, so Society members might call on her and her children. Here was a convert he could continue to disciple. It wasn't quite the same as having his own parish, but at least he wasn't required to ride away the next morning.

He felt ashamed that even in the rejoicing over the recovery of a lost lamb, his joy was less than complete. He wondered why God would have given him this desire for a people to shepherd if it was to remain unfulfilled.

And then the unaccustomed amount of self-analysis he had been undergoing lately led him to turn again to the Great Shepherd for guidance. In the empty chapel he knelt. "Lord, make me more useful for Thy service. I have prayed long for a place of service, but first do what You will to the server."

He went home still fearful of the vulnerability he had opened himself to, but he was sure he was on the right course.

The next morning, Catherine, back in the schoolroom, looked at the eleven eager faces in front of her. Well—seven eager, two cautious, and two bored. What did she most want to teach them in the short time she had with them? How could she best prepare them for life? How could she most clearly impart the love of God to them?

Three could barely form their letters; six read stumblingly; two were good readers for their age, but might be forced to leave school at any time as Isaiah Smithson had been. Then they would have very little exposure to books or to the Scriptures.

As she looked at them, longing to reach their minds and souls, she was filled with a new awareness of her love for them. And then she knew—she must reach them just as God had reached her—in the only way that one personality could reach another—with love.

She smiled at them. Eleven chubby, grubby faces smiled back. Well, nine smiled back; two were making faces at each other.

"Good morning, children. I am most anxious to hear what you have learned in my absence. Hettie, will you please read for us first."

Hettie stood, smoothed her apron, sniffled, and began reading, "'The eye of God is on them that do ill. Go not from me, O God, my God. The Lord will help them that cry to Him. My Son, if thy way is bad, see that you mend it.'"

"Thank you, Hettie." She called on three more to read aloud; then the scraping of little feet on the wooden floor told her it was time to vary the routine. "All right, class. You may turn to the syllabarium and copy out your letters." Primer pages rustled until all the children had before them a page of five columns of two-letter syllables that formed the basis of reading instruction. "And mind that you make your lines straight."

For a few minutes the heads bent over their slates, until a scraping sound told her someone was not applying his slate for its proper function. "William, you will stand in the corner for ten minutes, after which time I expect your writing instrument to work more smoothly." She had no more than dealt with that than a squeal from Kitty, the smallest girl, told her that Joshua had pulled her long braids again. "Joshua, please present yourself."

Discipline was not her favorite part of the job, but she struggled to put to rest her earlier visions of directing the children with nothing but the power of love as she held the birch rod before her. "Hold out your hands."

At such times she had to rely on the wisdom of John Wesley's instructions to his teachers:

> We must, by the grace of God, turn the bias from self-will, pride, anger, revenge, and love for the world, to lowliness, meekness, and the love of God. From the moment we perceive any of those evil roots springing up, it is our business immediately to check their growth, if we cannot root them out. As far as this can be done by mildness, softness, gentleness, certainly it should be done. But sometimes, these methods will not avail, and then we must correct with kind severity. For where tenderness will not remove the fault, he that spareth the rod, spoileth the child. To deny this is to give the lie to the God of truth and to suppose we can govern better than He.

Wesley's words gave her the courage to administer the full number of lashes. "You may take your seat and resume your work, Joshua." The students worked quietly, and Catherine prayed for the balance Wesley wanted them to achieve. He warned that some teachers may habitually lean to an extreme of being overly remiss or severe. If they gave children too much of their own will or needlessly and churlishly restrained them; if they used no punishment at all or more than was necessary, all their endeavors could be frustrated.

She pulled the watch from her waistband. The hands had barely moved since last she looked. "William, you may take your seat. And now, class, we shall read together. On the next page of your primer, please listen carefully and pronounce each word as I do."

Durial continued weak, mourning the loss of their child, and Ned stayed close to her side. Philip departed for a tour of Gloucestershire, and Catherine's students droned on. Duty and routine took over. Each morning brought the splash of cold water in her basin, the rumble of carriages on dry rocks, the scratch of styluses on slates. The Foundery looked as grim to her as when it was used only for metal forging.

Where were the birds' songs? Where were the roses? The scent of new-mown hay and the freshness after rain?

"Are You there, my God? Do You care? Are You still the loving Person who touched my heart and changed my life? Or have You too become only duty and routine?"

And in the stillness of her aching heart the answer came, "As I have been, so shall I be." God had promised help for the dry, dull times too, and so she must claim it and simply go on. She looked at her students.

"You may read, Joshua."

"Yes, Miss Perronet. 'Christ is the truth. Christ is the light. Christ is the way. Christ is my life . . .'"

At the end of two weeks, a feeble Durial was allowed to arise from her bed for a short time. Ned carried her to a lounge chair in the garden and tucked robes securely around her. Catherine was reading aloud to her sister-in-law from the *Meditations* of John Donne when they heard the clatter of horses' hooves on the driveway. For an instant Catherine's heart leaped—could it be their friend returning early from Gloucester? She had refused to dwell on the thought, even to admit it to her mind; but in the furthest recess of her heart she knew that much of the dryness of the past weeks could be laid to Philip's absence.

But the newcomer, although clad in the familiar black, was not her Philip but their brother Charl, just returned from a circuit to the north with Charles Wesley.

"Did you meet with success, Brother?" Catherine asked.

Charl removed his tricorn and ran his fingers through his hair. "I have never met with greater discord."

"Oh, Charl, were you treated rudely by the mob?" Durial asked with quick concern.

"No, no. We met little rowdyism. I speak of the Societies—of the preachers to be exact."

"Discord among the preachers?" Catherine couldn't believe her ears.

"First, there was the matter of James Wheatley—who was accused of embracing the doctrine of polygamy and, we were told, scandalized the Society by practicing it openly."

"Charl, was there any truth to such an accusation?"

"At the direction of John Wesley, his brother and I immediately set up an inquiry into the matter." Charl shook his head. "There was no polygamy, but that would perhaps have been easier to deal with. I heard Wheatley preach with my own ears. I cannot say whether he preached false doctrine or true, or any doctrine at all, but pure unmixed nonsense. Not one sentence did he utter that could do the least good to any soul.

"And there lies the weakest point of our Methodist system of preaching. The majority of those who fill the pulpits are working men who have abandoned their trade to follow what they believe to be their vocation, but without education or preparation or support, except from family or Society."

"What is to be done?" Catherine asked.

"Charles Wesley has declared that every preacher must work at his own trade or business during the week, preparing his sermons as he finds time and delivering them on Sundays in the neighboring chapels. This way they will at least not lose touch with the common man."

"Well, then, it seems the matter has been taken in hand."

"Yes, but that was not all. We encountered amongst the more prominent of the preachers a spirit of disloyalty to the Church of England that horrified Charles, whose allegiance to the Anglican faith knows no bounds."

"Oh, Charl, not more separatism talk?"

"Of a truth, the remedy is simple, and more and more of our harassed preachers are availing themselves of it. For the sum of sixpence they are furnished with a license which puts them under the protection of the law. Once they are recognized as 'protestant dissenters,' they are no longer at the mercy of the mob. And a similar license will protect their meetinghouses from wreckers and incendiaries. We are beating our heads against the wall in refusing this way."

"But to leave the church . . . ," Catherine said in horror.

Charl laughed. "Cath, you sound like Charles Wesley. He said he should rather see his brother in his grave than a dissenter. But it will come to it in time."

Catherine went alone into the garden—alone to consider this further unhappy news. Dissension and faulty standards among the Society preachers, widespread agitation for separatism. What were the answers? On every hand trouble was invading the world of the Methodist Society—what had seemed to her the best of all possible worlds. And Catherine felt afraid. She had conquered her fear of horses. But this new fear was much worse—fear of the future was like walking down a long, dark tunnel without a candle. Without assurance of God's guidance, she could feel no assurance of His caring. If no caring, did He then truly provide salvation?

No! She put the question aside as one that came directly from the enemy. She would not doubt that. She would choose to believe, no matter how little she felt the closeness of the Savior at times.

With that determination she suddenly knew what she would do. There was one place where she had always felt closer to God than any other. She would go for a walk in the woods.

She ran to her room for her half-boots and a shawl. Telling Audrey where she was going, she hurried out again into the day, which now seemed brighter. Once in the woods the beauty began to seep into her soul—a greenness of trees, a trill of birdsong. And her spirits rose higher, as if the trees that shut the world from view behind her shut out the problems too. Here were no rowdy crowds, no dissenting preachers, no disobedient schoolchildren, no poverty-stricken families, no disappointed loves. Here there was a coloring of flowers, a sparkle of water, a warmth of sun. One could not possibly doubt the personal love of a God who created such a world.

Catherine felt her inner doubts, fears, and anxieties slip away. She knew they would come back later when she returned to the real world, but for now she could laugh, thank God, and shout hosanna.

Had anyone been watching her, however, they would have had no idea all this was going on inside the outwardly composed young woman who walked down the wooded path, stopping occasionally to pick a specimen for her wildflower press. An especially lovely hawthorn tree brought back to mind the Maying she and her companions had watched on the Kentish village green. She decided to collect a sprig for her book.

The hawthorn branch was just beyond her reach. She stretched her hand to the delicate cluster of berries that would soon turn red, but even when she stood on her tiptoes, they eluded her grasp. Then a gentle breeze, just a small stirring of the air, brought the branch into her hands.

She picked it gladly, freely, as it had been given to her, and savored its beauty in joy. At that moment she understood. She had thought she must reach God's will and had strained her arms and stood on tiptoe to grasp it. But the truth was that He reached down to her. Just as the heaven-sent breeze had placed the hawthorn berries in her hand, so God, in His reaching down to her, had placed and would place all good things in her life according to His perfect way.

The shadows were falling long across the path. It was time to return. With only the slightest reluctance, she turned her steps back to the world with its challenges and opportunities. "Help me to view them as such, my God, rather than as threats or burdens. Help me, I ask, to serve You more gladly. As gladly as You gave me the hawthorn blossom."

At first the faint calling of her name sounded as a rustling in the trees, coming so immediately after her prayer that it seemed as if the voice of God were calling her. And then she thought she had imagined it, recalling her childhood experience when her brother's voice had come to the little girl lost in the woods. But on the fourth call, she knew it was not the wind, not her Creator, not her imagination. It was a very human male voice. And on the fifth call, she identified the caller. With a cry of gladness, she turned and ran up the path to Philip.

8

*P*hillip stood on the path in a shaft of late afternoon sunlight. For a moment Catherine felt as if she were seeing him for the first time—his striking height, his endearing thinness, his fleeting smile. During the past two weeks she had thought of him with confused emotions because she hadn't the slightest idea of whether he was thinking of her at all. Indeed, it was impossible ever to guess what he thought, much less what he felt. And now, except for a light in his blue eyes that she hoped she wasn't imagining, his chiseled features were a perfect mask—a barrier between the man inside and the world outside.

Catherine had become part of his outside world; would she ever get inside behind the mask? She would like to have thrown her arms around him in welcome, but instead offered him a composed smile. "How pleased I am that you are returned. Tell me about your journey."

They walked up the path toward the house together. "I met with my friend George Whitefield," he told her. "He was desperately ill on his voyage from America, but he is recovering. He hopes to accompany Lady Huntingdon to London in a few days."

"And what of your services? Had you success?"

"Yes, but the most remarkable victory over Satan was scored before I left the Foundery." Now, as he talked about his work, the stiffness gave way to animation. "Have you heard of the conversion of Mrs. Smithson? The night before I left, she wandered in off the street while I was preaching—"

"Smithson?"

"Yes. I instructed the sisters to call on her. Do you know if any have? Her tale was absolutely remarkable. She was returning from a bagnio where she had sought to sell herself for the sake of buying bread for her children—"

"Had she red hair?"

"It seems so, if I recall—"

"Oh, Philip!" Catherine so forgot herself as to take his arm. "It must be the same. Isaiah Smithson was my pupil, but he had to quit and go to sweeping when his father lost his job. And you say she found the Lord?"

"Indeed, it was a remarkable conversion. She seemed truly a new person."

"Philip, we must help that family. Do you think the Society might—"

"Lend to an unemployed man whose children sweep? I believe the Society lending policies to be sounder than that. The Society will lend up to twenty shillings, but the sum must be repaid within three months. It seems most unlikely Smithson could meet those terms."

"But we must do something."

"Indeed we must. Will you call on her with me?"

Catherine readily agreed, and they continued on up the path. She saw no reason to let go of the arm she held.

And the following day Catherine clung to the same arm as protection from the squalor around her. Chitty Lane off Tottenham Court Road ran past a row of dilapidated houses that had been turned into one-room dwellings. Children with pock-marked faces and emaciated limbs played in the gutters, which obviously were disposal systems for all manner of waste.

"Catherine, I should not have asked you to accompany me. I had no idea—," Philip began.

"I believe we had this conversation once before, sir. Surely this is what our Lord had in mind when He reminded us, 'As ye have done it unto the least of these.'"

It seemed impossible to Catherine that such a pocket of misery could exist in the very center of London, almost equidistant between the purity of the Foundery and Aldersgate Street to the east, and the elegance of Mayfair and Park Lane to the west. She turned her eyes away from the sight of a scraggly dog shaking a rat to death and resisted the impulse to put her hand over her nose.

An urchin directed them down a mud path to an unpainted door hanging crooked on its hinges, and then he held out his filthy hand for a farthing. It wasn't the dirt on the hand that shocked Catherine. He had a running sore on his inflamed palm. "Philip, if that isn't treated, he'll lose his hand."

The stench from the street followed them into the Smithson home where at least there was some semblance of order, some attempt to keep the filth at bay with sweeping and scrubbing. With a toddler clinging to her skirt, Elmira Smithson was at work over a stack of linen, ironing with alternating flatirons kept hot on the hearth.

Elmira's greeting seemed cheerful beyond all possibility in her circumstances. "The good Jesus you told us about 'asn't left me for one minute," she assured Philip. "And the Methody sisters bring two loads o' wash. More'n I've 'ad in as many weeks afore."

But her accounting of her blessings was interrupted by a fretful cry from a pallet in a dark corner of the room.

"Are you awake, Isey? We've visitors."

"Miss Perronet!" The fussy voice changed to a whoop of joy.

"Isaiah! I didn't see you there. Are you ill?"

"'S me feet. I got stuck an' the sweep built a fire under me. I wasn't a'feared—t'weren't that. I were stuck."

The sight of Isaiah's badly blistered feet brought tears to

Catherine's eyes. His mother had attempted to soothe the fever in her son's feet with cool rags. "Have you no salve?" Catherine asked.

Elmira shook her head.

"I shall bring you some first thing in the morning," Catherine promised. "Now, young man, where is the primer I loaned you? Let us see if you have remembered what I labored so hard to teach you."

Isaiah produced the book, in much better condition than Catherine had dared hope for, from under his pallet. They spent half an hour reviewing the answers to the picture catechism while Philip instructed Mrs. Smithson from the Bible.

"And what of your husband? Has he found work?" Philip asked as they prepared to take their leave.

"Da's in the Fleet," Isaiah said, before his mother could answer.

"The Fleet?" Catherine couldn't have kept the horror out of her voice if she'd tried. The Fleet was the largest of London's debtors' prisons, notorious for its dirt, debauchery, and harsh treatment of prisoners—and for the hopelessness of gaining release.

"'E owed Mr. Pinchbeck two quid. When 'e couldn't pay, ol' Pinchy swore out a complaint, swore 'e owed 'im twenty. 'Course they would a taken 'im for the two just the same. Tha's why I went to the bagnio; it's the only place I could think of to earn that kinda money. But they didn't even want laundry done by the loiks of me—let alone any other service."

"For twenty pounds he could be freed?" Philip asked.

Mrs. Smithson shook her head. "There's the garnish for the jailer and the warden and the guard. Upwards of fifty quid, I should think."

"Fifty pounds!" Catherine was thunderstruck. She knew the graft and corruption in the prison system was unconscionable, but fifty pounds amounted to the yearly salary of a well-to-do man. It was far beyond anything Smithson or any of his family could ever hope to raise. Even Catherine, who would gladly have paid his release, couldn't imagine where such a sum could be found.

The toddler began to whimper for some of the thin gruel heating on the hearth beside the flatirons. Catherine was glad she had brought a basket of bread. Before she and Philip left, they prayed with the family in a small circle around Isaiah's mat. "I will return with medicine for your feet, Isaiah," Catherine promised from the doorway.

"You must not come here alone," Philip told her sternly when they were back on their way to the Foundery. "It's not safe. I shall accompany you tomorrow."

And he did, as soon as her class was dismissed the next day. And the next as well. Catherine was pleased that Isaiah's blisters were responding to the calves' jelly salve, but she feared having him fully recovered and going back to sweeping chimneys again. "Philip, I've been thinking about Isaiah. I can't supply the money to get his father out of prison, but I can spare enough to keep him in the charity school."

"What do you have in mind?"

"I'm not sure yet—maybe supplying the family with the amount of food he could have bought with his earnings as a sweep. If it's done through the Society, surely they would accept it."

"That is most generous of you, Catherine. I should like to share the responsibility with you."

"Oh, but, Philip—forgive me, but you have so little."

"On the contrary, I have so much. A visit such as this makes me conscious of it. Please pardon me if I seem presumptuous when I say that it is my observation that children reared by well-to-do parents accept what comes to them as a right—demand it even. One who has received everything from another's open-handedness learns appreciation quickly. And since there is nothing I can do to repay those who gave to me, I must give to others."

Catherine nodded. "The theological implications seem boundless."

"God's grace to us all—unmerited favor, you mean?"

"Yes, and adoption—we are all adopted into God's family and made heirs by His love."

For a moment it seemed to Catherine that Philip was considering his next movement very carefully. Then, decidedly, for the first time in their acquaintanceship, he offered his arm without her making the first move.

That small linking action stayed with Catherine throughout the evening. Later that night, when reading in her green vellum volume of John Donne by the light of a branched candelabra, she came upon his "Meditation 17." But she found it impossible to think of mankind in general, as the grave image of Philip Ferrar fixed itself in her mind's eye.

"No man is an island entire of itself." Ah, here was the part she looked for. Philip was such a remote island, and she had no barque to reach him. With a sigh she returned to her reading. "If a clod be washed away by the sea, Europe is the less, as well as if a promontory were, as well as if a manor of thy friend's or of thine own were. Any man's death diminishes me. . . ."

"And any child's pain," she added. She wished she could take all the urchins in London under her wing, put salve on their sores, teach them to read. But at least she could minister to the one God had placed directly in her path. Tomorrow she would approach Elmira Smithson about Isaiah's returning to school.

But the next morning Catherine's day presented a full schedule of duties before she could visit the Smithsons. John Wesley was now returned to London, living in his rooms over the Foundery, and he would be preaching at five o'clock in the morning, which meant that Catherine must arrive early to be assured of a good seat.

It had been many weeks since John Wesley had filled his

pulpit, and yet when he stood before them, it was as if he had never been away. In spite of his forty-six years, he appeared fresh, his eyes bright and piercing and his long hair still a rich auburn. But most compelling was the intelligence, energy, and love he radiated to all around him.

He launched quickly into his sermon on Matthew 25:43: "I was . . . sick, and in prison, and ye visited me not." And he spoke eloquently of love for one's neighbors, love that endures everything, that feeds an enemy and gives him drink, "thus continually heaping coals of fire—of melting love—upon his head."

Wesley continued, speaking more specifically about prison visitation, and gradually Catherine became sensible of her own negligence. Never had she visited a prisoner. She didn't even know how to go about it.

Then Wesley concluded the service by introducing Sarah Peters who had come to the Foundery looking for volunteers to visit prisons. "This very week in the Fleet," Miss Peters told the congregation, "there are ten malefactors under sentence of death who would be glad of any friends who could go and pray with them."

Quailing inwardly, Catherine joined the band of workers around Sarah Peters at the side of the altar after the service. "I shall go with you," Catherine pledged.

She was still shaking inwardly when she turned to leave and saw Philip among the volunteers. Then she knew she could do it.

But that afternoon when they met Sarah Peters outside the Fleet, Catherine had second thoughts, even with the support of Philip, her headmaster Silas Told, and two other Society members.

"There are three large wards on the common side," Miss Peters explained. "Here the prisoners are obliged to lie on the floor if they cannot furnish themselves with bedding—this is hired out at a cost of a shilling per week. There are also two smaller wards, including an exceedingly noisome one for women. A number of rooms on the master's side are let out at indefinite charges to occupants who can pay the warden. In some rooms persons who are sick of different distempers are obliged to lie together or on the floor and must pay two shillings, ten pence per week for such lodging. But," she hastened to add, "you may be assured we shall in no wise go near cases of small-pox or similar contagion."

As Miss Peters turned to lead the way to the prison gate, Silas Told asked, "I have been given to understand that even prisoners for debt must pay garnish to the jailers."

"Yes, that is true. James Oglethorpe who heads a reform committee has made two reports to Parliament on these abuses. We still hope for amelioration. But at present, when taken into custody and sent to the Fleet, every prisoner is expected to pay a total of five pounds, sixteen shillings, and four pence in fees. This is divided between the warden, the tipstaff, and the clerk of the judge who ordered the committal."

"But what if they can't pay?" Catherine could think only of Mrs. Smithson's happiness over being given a pitiful pile of laundry whereby to earn a few shillings.

"When the miserable wretch has worn out the charity of his friends and used up the money raised from the sale of his clothes and bedding and has eaten his last allowance of provisions, he soon grows weak for want of food, with the symptoms of a hectic fever. When he is no longer able to stand, if he can raise three pence to pay the fee of the common nurse of the prison, he obtains the liberty of being carried into the sick ward and lingers on for a month or two on charity rations, and then dies."

"But can nothing be done about it?"

"Oglethorpe's committee is sending petitions to Parliament, and there is hope of Parliament passing ameliorating legislation. But in the meantime, it seems most fit that we should strive for the souls of these unhappy prisoners. There is little we can do for them here but prepare them for a better world to come. Let us proceed."

Sarah Peters, a seasoned warrior in this arena of graft and corruption, approached the Ordinary, a Mr. Taylor who, but for the fact that he stood outside the walls, looked far meaner and more disreputable than any of his prisoners. "You shall not obstruct our entrance today, Mr. Taylor. The God of all compassion shall make an entrance for us so that our acts of compassion and mercy may continue." When she accompanied her bold words with the clink of bribe money, the group was allowed to pass.

Catherine thought she was prepared for the fetid air and squalid, verminous surroundings. But as the great iron bar clanked into place across the heavy oak door behind them, and she knew herself locked inside with desperate murderers and felons as well as with the malignant diseases that ravaged the rag-covered bodies she saw on every side of her, she felt panic.

"You needn't do this, Catherine. Shall I take you home?" With the sound of Philip's voice, the terror subsided.

"I can do it, Philip. But stay by me."

He ducked his head in a nod of assurance, and she was almost sure she saw a flicker of an encouraging smile cross his face. It was for Catherine as if a brilliant light filled the murky room.

But she had no leisure to consider her own feelings, as the determined Miss Peters shepherded their small party forward to the cell of a prisoner named Lancaster. The turnkey opened the barred door and then closed it behind them.

Sarah encouraged Lancaster to tell his story. He was very young, just above twenty, Catherine judged, yet he told of having lived a life of great wickedness, including having robbed the Foundery of all its brass and candlesticks. "But shortly I shall be with Jesus in paradise. This morning, about five o'clock, the Son of Righteousness arose in my dark cell, and I am now so full of God and Heaven that I am like a barrel of new wine ready to burst for vent."

The visitors joined him in praising God, and Lancaster

gave praise for Miss Peters and her workers who had shown him the way to God.

They visited another cell where six prisoners, all under sentence of death, seemed assured of their acceptance by the Savior. The workers were about to leave when another prisoner, having bribed the turnkey, entered the cell. His sullen face showed he had not come to praise God with them. "Come to scoff at us, are ye? Come to turn us into milksops 'afore we face the hangman? I'll none of your pap!"

Philip stepped forward and said softly, "My friend, let us tell you what we have come to tell any who will hear."

The prisoner muttered, but seemed less violent, so Philip continued, "We have come to invite you to the Lord Jesus. To invite you to come as a lost and undone sinner because Jesus is the sinner's only friend. Jesus, the King of Heaven, laid down His life for you."

As Philip spoke, the man's countenance softened. But there was time for no more. The iron door clanked open, and the warden stood before them, filling the passage with his straddle-legged stance, a fearsome sight in his heavy boots and leather jerkin, with black, greasy hair falling to his shoulders. He grasped his sword hilt with a broad hand. "The report has been made, and the dead warrant just come down. Four of you are ordered for execution. Look to your souls."

As the visitors were ushered from the cell, Sarah Peters assured the condemned men she would come again before their execution.

They were almost to the outer door, passing the largest and, therefore, dirtiest and noisiest of the common cells, when Catherine recognized a woman in the corridor. "Elmira, I didn't think to see you here." She hurried to Mrs. Smithson.

"I must come to bring Dick 'is loaf." She held up a small hunk of bread. "Some weeks 'tis all 'e 'as to eat if the rations is withheld."

Catherine dug in the pocket she wore tied under her skirt

for a coin with which to bribe the turnkey. "Allow me a few minutes longer with my friend."

He jerked his head in assent.

Philip joined her as they stood beside the cell bars with Mrs. Smithson. As unobtrusively as possible she slipped the loaf through to her husband and introduced Catherine and Philip.

Their reception was less than gracious. "What the devil possesses you, Elmiry? Bringin' canters to see me. I 'ope you've not been among the Methodists! I'd sacrifice what's left of my soul rather than you shall go among those miscreants." He shook his fist through the bars. "You're the ones wot filled Isey's 'ead so full of larnin' 'e ain't no good t' sweep."

Elmira moved the visitors to the other side of the passage. "It's th' gin talkin'. 'E didn't use to drink bad, but there's naught else to do 'ere."

"Gin? But where do they get it?" Catherine asked.

Philip answered. "What isn't smuggled in under the skirts of female visitors is sold right here."

"What? In the gaol?"

"I have read some of the accounts of Oglethorpe's committee. Upwards of thirty gin shops operate inside the Fleet alone."

Back in her carriage in the fresh air, it seemed to Catherine that the sun had never shown more golden, the flowers bloomed more brightly, nor the trees waved greener in the breeze. She took in great gulps of air, as if she had been holding her breath the entire time she was behind the high stone walls of the Fleet. "Oh, I don't think I've ever truly appreciated freedom before!"

The men agreed with her. Each determined to work harder in his own field—Philip the preacher, who sought to free people from the prison of sin, and Silas Told the schoolmaster, who fought the prison of ignorance. But the metaphor Catherine was living in was the sunshine and the light that had dawned in her world in the darkness of the prison. And that light was Philip

Ferrar. For weeks now he had been central in her thinking—as a dear friend, a special person in the Society work. But now, from the blackness of the Fleet had dawned the light of love.

He had said nothing any gentleman of casual acquaintance might not have said, but the simple fact of his presence had been all. As she tried to make sense of this, to understand what it would mean in the days ahead, the darkness of the prison experience offered another metaphor. She recognized the inability to see into the future as a kind of blindness. "We see through a glass darkly," as the Scripture said. But now she realized that God had so ordained this in order to develop faith— that one must rely on the Heavenly Guide as a blind man relies on an earthly guide. But someday it would all be known, and all knowledge would be as clear as knowledge of the past now was. Clearer, really, because His perfect light would illumine the whole.

She shuddered at the thought of what life without God would be like—like one physically blind walking without a guide. She had experienced a little of that in the days after her crushing disappointment, when she had lost faith in God's guidance. She had been blind, and in a way, she still was. She had no more ability to see the future than before, but she did have faith in her Guide.

*C*atherine hoped that the tall, quiet man on the carriage seat beside her would have a place in that future. The thought of his being taken from her as Charles Wesley had been was more than she could bear.

"Shall you mind that very much?"

Philip's words so nearly echoing those in her head made Catherine jump. "I beg your pardon. What did you say?"

"I said I have been commanded to bring you and Edward to Lady Huntingdon's drawing room to hear Whitefield preach tomorrow afternoon." He turned his head away from Silas Told, who was now reading beside him, and spoke quietly. "Charles and Sally Wesley shall be there. I thought you would want to know."

"You are thoughtful to warn me, but I shall be fine. And you?"

For a moment he looked puzzled. Then the level blue eyes so close to hers cleared. "Absolutely fine."

The next day gathering storm clouds darkened patches of London's sky as Catherine and Edward Perronet and Philip Ferrar set out from the Foundery for Park Lane. It was the first time the three of them had traveled together since their circuit ride and almost the first time Edward had been abroad since Durial's desperate illness. So whatever the clouds might do to the sky, the renewal of old times and the strong sense of companionship in the carriage could not be dimmed.

The crush of coaches with armorial bearings outside number 14 Park Lane facing on Hyde Park told the new arrivals that they were hardly alone in their obedience to the countess's summons. A select circle of aristocratic acquaintances had frequently accompanied the countess to Whitefield's sermons in London churches years before; but Lady Huntingdon's long retirement from society after her husband's death and her own bouts of illness had ended these excursions—until now. Whitefield's return and the renewal of her energies coincided in perfect timing.

At the top of the pillared portico the door was opened by a liveried butler who announced their arrival, but once into the high-ceilinged, marble-floored reception room, they made no more progress. The aged widow of the Duke of Marlborough stood in front of them, clasping the hand of her hostess. "My dear Lady Huntingdon, I really do feel so sensibly all your kindness and attention that I must accept your obliging invitation to hear Mr. Whitefield, though I am still suffering from the effects of a severe ague." She waved a white lace handkerchief as supporting evidence.

"My dear Duchess."

The duchess not only outranked Lady Huntingdon—she was also the only woman Catherine knew of who could out-talk her. "Your concern for my improvement in religious knowledge is very obliging. God knows we all need mending, and none more than myself."

"Won't you come into the drawing room, Your Grace?"

The duchess took two steps at her hostess's bidding and then paused again. "The Duchess of Ancaster, Lady Townshend, and Lady Cobham were exceedingly pleased with many observations in Mr. Whitefield's sermon at St. Sepulchre's Church, which made me lament ever since that I did not hear it, as it might have been the means of doing me some good—for *good*, alas! I do want."

"As we all do, Your Grace. And there is the ill-used Lady Anne Frankland." The countess pointed her fan in the direction of a wan-looking woman. "The poor thing is so unhappy in her new marriage. To think that a great-grandson of Oliver Cromwell could abuse his wife so. Do see if you can comfort her." With that, Lady Huntingdon dispatched her garrulous guest and turned to Catherine. "So you are come. I have been in town these three days. You must call on me more often."

"I should be happy to, My Lady. Of late I have been much engaged in calling on the sick and imprisoned."

"Yes, indeed. Very worthy work. You must tell me more of it. But we must also carry our message to the wealthy and aristocratic, if the work is to be a lasting one. The influence of money and society is too much overlooked by John Wesley."

The arrival at that moment of two women sumptuously clad in ribbed silk embroidered with silver thread, their skirts spread wide over flattened hoops, proved the success of the countess's campaign.

"The Dowager Duchess of Buckingham," the butler announced. "And the Duchess of Queensberry."

"Well, Selina, I have brought Eleanor with me to hear your favorite preacher," the Dowager Duchess announced with a flip of her ivory fan.

The Duchess of Queensberry managed to nod at her introduction while still keeping her nose in the air. "La, I am exceedingly fatigued. I trust he will not tire me beyond endurance."

Catherine and her escorts started to follow the newcomers up the stairs to the drawing room, but at the entrance of another party the countess halted them and made her own announcement even before the butler could. "Catherine, this is Sally Wesley; Charles you already know." She dismissed the husband.

"You young ladies are to become great friends." And with that decree she waved them up the stairs.

But Catherine could not so easily dispense with the arrival of Charles Wesley. Her first glimpse of the glowing brown eyes and fair features most frequently described as "angelic," which had so long held preeminence in Catherine's heart and mind, made her catch her breath. But a second, more-considered look told her that the far-from-classic features of the gaunt man beside Charles had become much dearer to her.

"I am most happy to meet you, Miss Perronet," Sally Wesley acknowledged the introduction, as the ladies led the way up the stairs. "Your brother was so kind in supporting our cause in Garth."

"Yes, Ned has told me of your wedding. I am happy to meet you too." And as she spoke the words, Catherine realized how very much she meant them. Sally was short and viva-cious, with dark curls bouncing beneath her lace cap and snapping dark eyes that made her appear even younger than her twenty-one years. And every time those black eyes fell on her husband of three months, they bespoke how much she loved him.

They barely had time to find seats in the green and rose room when the countess called on Mr. and Mrs. Charles Wesley to provide music for her guests. Sally, in a flowered dimity dress over a pink petticoat, looked the perfect part of the happy new bride as she seated herself at the harpsichord and filled the room with its delicate music. And then her husband stood by her side as together they sang: "Rejoice, the Lord is King; Your Lord and king adore! / Rejoice, give thanks, and sing and triumph evermore: / Lift up your heart, lift up your voice! Rejoice, again I say, rejoice!"

It was obvious that the musicians were rejoicing in their life together and in the grace of which they sang. The hearts of their hearers were lifted with them. Sunshine streamed through the tall windows of the room as they sang. Catherine's heart could sing along with the musicians—Charles and Sally were so right for each other! After all her struggles over God's guidance, it was still impossible to know where He was leading her; but that these two were right for each other was indisputable. She must simply trust that God had an equally right answer in store for her life. And seeing that God had led so graciously in the lives of others could help her believe that He would make His way plain to her.

Then George Whitefield stood at the end of the room beside the east windows. He was of middle height, slender, fair, and good-looking except for a squint in one eye. Nothing about his appearance would predispose his audience to pick out this young man as the one who had brought thousands to Christ on both sides of the Atlantic.

But when he began to speak, they understood. Remarkably, he could speak rapidly and yet have every word distinctly heard. "We are all dead in sin and cannot save ourselves. We are saved by the free grace of God, without the assistance of good works which have no share in the matter, though it is impossible for us to have this free grace applied to us without its being followed by good works.

"Good works are, however, the sure tokens of our being born again. . . . Everybody that pleases may obtain this free grace by simply praying for it. It is therefore by faith in Christ alone that we are saved, not by our good works."

Clouds alternated with sunshine as Whitefield continued to build the solid doctrinal foundation on which he based every sermon. In a moment when a shadow crossed the room, he stretched out his arm. "See that emblem of human life! It passed for a moment and concealed the brightness of heaven from our view. But it is gone! And where will you be, my hearers, when your lives are passed away like that dark cloud?

"O my dear friends, I see you sitting attentive, with your eyes fixed on this poor, unworthy preacher. In a few days we shall all meet at the Judgment Seat of Christ, and every eye shall behold the Judge! With a voice whose call you must abide and answer, He will inquire whether on earth you strove to enter in at the strait gate. Whether you were supremely devoted to God. Whether your hearts were absorbed in Him."

Now the sun was gone, the room dark, and thunder rumbled in the distance. "My blood runs cold when I think how many of you will seek to enter in and shall not be able. What plea can you make before the Judge of the whole earth?"

The storm was almost overhead. In the eerie light of the thunderclouds, George Whitefield held his arms aloft and cried, "O sinner! By all your hopes of happiness I beseech you to repent. Let not the wrath of God be awakened! Let not the fires of eternity be kindled against you."

Forked lightning streaked past the windows. "See there! It is a glance from the angry eye of Jehovah. Hark—" He lifted his finger and paused. A tremendous crash of thunder shook the room. As it died away, the preacher's deep voice spoke from the semidarkness. "It was the voice of the Almighty as He passed by in anger!"

Whitefield covered his face with his hands and fell to his knees in silent prayer until the storm subsided. When the sun shone again in a few minutes, the windows reflected a magnificent rainbow. The preacher rose and pointed at it. "Look upon the rainbow and praise Him who made it. Very beautiful it is in the brightness thereof. It compasseth the heavens about with glory, and the hands of the Most High have bended it."

It was several moments before anyone moved in the room. At last Lord Bolingbroke rose, shook out the lace ruffles beneath the wide cuffs of his green velvet coat, and crossed the room to the speaker. "Sir, I am much moved by your address. Will you call upon me tomorrow morning?"

"I would be much honored, My Lord."

It seemed that Bolingbroke's stamp of approval was what all were waiting for, as now all the guests surged around the speaker. Lord Chesterfield, godfather to the young Earl of

Huntingdon, the countess's son, shook Whitefield's hand. "Sir, I will not tell you what I shall tell others—how I approve of you." He stayed for some time, affably conversing with the preacher.

But the outspoken Dowager Duchess of Buckingham was less enthusiastic as she took leave of her hostess. "I thank Your Ladyship for the information concerning the Methodist preacher. But I find his doctrine most repulsive. It is strongly tinctured with impertinence and disrespect for his superiors."

She turned toward all the room and tapped her walking stick on the parquet floor. "It is monstrous to be told that you have a heart as sinful as the common wretches that crawl upon the earth. I find this highly offensive and insulting. I cannot but wonder that Your Ladyship should relish any sentiments so much at variance with high rank and good breeding." With a toss of her head, she exited, the still-fatigued Duchess of Queensberry following in her wake.

As the noble guests made their departure and the room became easier to move about in, Catherine gravitated to Sally Wesley's side, wishing to compliment her on her excellent musicianship. But they had exchanged only a few words before the guest of honor joined them. "And how is the excellent Mrs. Wesley?" Whitefield asked.

"Very well, sir. I thank you."

"And how are you getting along in the book I gave you?"

"Exceeding well." She turned to Catherine. "Mr. Whitefield made me a wedding present of William Law's *A Serious Call to a Devout and Holy Life*."

"It is a gift I never tire of giving to others, for I never forget the great longing I had to possess a copy." Catherine was especially interested in Whitefield's words, as she recalled Philip having told her that the book and its author had a great influence on his life. "I was just leaving for my first term at Oxford," Whitefield continued, "when I called on a friend who kept Gloucester's best bookshop. He showed me the brand-new book which had just arrived that day from London, but allowed me to hold it for a few minutes only, lest my grubby fingers spoil the calf. In those brief moments, though, I read enough to fire me. I still recall the passage: 'He therefore is the devout man who lives no longer to his own will, or to the sway and spirit of the world, but to the sole will of God; who considers God in everything, who serves God in everything, who makes all the parts of his common life, parts of piety, by doing everything in the name of God. . . . . '"

"That precise passage provided the recipe I followed for salvation," Charles Wesley said, as he joined them. "Law was counselor-in-chief to both my brother and myself during the years of our legal night. We often walked from Oxford to London to talk to him. His book convinced me of the exceeding height and breadth and depth of the love of God. The light flowed in so mightily upon my soul that everything appeared in a new view, and I cried to God for help."

The artist Loggan, who at Tunbridge Wells had declared his desire to hear more of the countess's doctrine, and the poet Lord Lyttelton had joined them in time to hear the last statement. "And reading that dissenting fellow's book changed your life? Remarkable!" said Loggan.

"The book and its author. They convinced me of the absolute impossibility of being half a Christian. I determined, through His grace, to be all devoted to God, to give Him my soul, my body, and my substance."

"But what did the fellow say to bring on such a determination?" Loggan asked.

Wesley returned Loggan's bow. "With respect to an inward means of atonement, or reconciliation to God, Mr. Law declared his unequivocal belief that through the body and blood of our Lord Jesus Christ alone, and by means of His suffering on the cross solely, mankind can be delivered from a state of sin and misery. That was the good news I had sought for years."

Lord Lyttelton made a deep bow accompanied by a flourish of his green velvet coat skirts. "That's William Law, you say? I once took up his book at a friend's house. I was so fascinated I could not go to rest until I had finished it. You can well imagine I was not a little astonished to find that one of the finest books ever written had been penned by a crack-brained enthusiast. Oh," Lord Lyttelton surveyed the circle to whom he spoke, "I daresay, that wasn't very tactful of me, was it?"

Wesley laughed. "Don't give it another thought; if crack-brained were the worst we were ever called, we should be remarkably complimented. But I believe much of Law's greatness lies in the fact that his sensitivity to logic is as marked as his sensitivity to conscience. Many of our number may be crack-brained, but I don't believe the term applicable to Mr. Law."

The poet bowed, and the silver thread on his coat shone in the light now streaming in the windows. "Perhaps that is why the book had such a powerful effect upon Dr. Johnson. I recall he told me he had become a sort of lax *talker* against religion, for he did not much *think* against it. He said this lasted till he went to Oxford and there took up Law's *Serious Call*, expecting to find it a dull book as such books generally are. 'But I found Law quite an overmatch for me; and this was the first occasion of my thinking in earnest of religion after I became capable of rational inquiry.' I believe I have his words exactly, as they made a profound impression upon my mind."

The conversation then became general and the Perronet party left a few minutes later, with Sally expressing her warm desire that she and Catherine should meet and visit more during the Wesleys' stay in London.

The very next afternoon, just after Catherine had dismissed her students to their noon meal, Sally saw her in the courtyard and called, "Do come up to John's rooms; he has begged that Charles and I make free of them while we're here." Sally led the way to Wesley's apartment and prepared tea for them in the large ivory and blue teapot made especially for John Wesley by Josiah Wedgewood. Catherine read the inscription on the pot:

Be present at our table, Lord,
Be here and everywhere ador'd;
These creatures bless and grant that we
May feast in paradise with Thee.

Sally poured the tea into little handleless dishes. "Oh, how good it is to be in a well-appointed house. I so long to set up housekeeping."

"Have you and Charles no place of your own?" Catherine tried to keep the surprise out of her voice.

"Alas, no. We have been riding circuit."

"On your honeymoon?" And this time Catherine made no attempt to hide her shock.

"Do not misunderstand. I'm not complaining. I'm most eager to share in my husband's work. And always we have the most sweet fellowship in the sacrament and in prayer. I could ask for nothing more, truly." She paused. "It is just that some-times the circumstances have been rather, er—uncomfortable."

Such gentle understatement aroused Catherine's sense of humor, and soon the tea was cooling in the dishes while they exchanged stories of their circuit-riding experiences. ". . . and then my mare dropped a shoe, which occasioned so much loss of time that we could not ride across the sands, but were obliged to go round through a miserable road. And then our guide lost his way, so that we arrived at the ferry too late for the last cross-ing . . ." Sally paused for a sip of tea while Catherine told of their near-disastrous crossing of the flooded river.

Then Sally took up the conversation. "The next day Charles was preaching to nearly three thousand when the press-gang came and seized one of the hearers. They even tried to take Charles, but he told them that as a duly ordained minister he was acting under protection of the king's law, and they left him alone."

Catherine then contributed her experience with the mili-tary in Canterbury.

"I do not believe Satan likes our work," Sally said. "But a higher One protects us. We were in a Society meeting in a home in Camborne when a member cried out, 'We will not stay here; we will go to Lefroy's house.' That house was in quite a different part of the town, but we all rose up and went, though none of us knew why. Soon after we were gone, a spark fell into a barrel of gunpowder, which was in the next room to the one we had vacated, and blew up the house."

"Such a story builds my faith. I have wrestled long with the matter of God's guidance in our lives."

"And have you reached a conclusion?"

"I am certain He guides . . . if we but have the faith to follow. I think it is now a matter of understanding His perfect timing. Perhaps it is just that I am too impatient." Catherine spread her hands in a helpless gesture.

Sally laughed and took Catherine's hand. "Oh, how good it is to talk to one who shares my feelings! I have no answers either, but so many questions. And I do know that holding on to the good times—all the times God has answered and fulfilled His promises—has gotten me through the bad times.

"Like the evening Charles was preaching in a barn when he began to sink out of sight before my very eyes. I never knew worse fear. I thought he was to be taken away from me right there. It turned out that the barn had been built on a marsh, and the weight of the crowd made the floor sink. No one was hurt, and we continued with a glorious service in the field. That night many even fainted under the sense of God's love."

Then Sally laughed again and finished her story in a hushed voice. "And that night in the inn, the mattress collapsed right through the bedstead, and we were obliged to sleep on the floor."

Catherine had promised Durial she would not be late, so the women parted, promising to have many more such visits.

But that was not to be; for when Catherine reached Greenwich, she found Durial headachy and fretful and still struggling to carry on with the housework. For many days Catherine's time was fully consumed and allowed no leisure for anything but duties at school and home. Even her resolution to visit Elmira Smithson had to be postponed.

Philip, however, was carrying forth his program of prison visitation with success. He had gone back every day since that initial visit to pray with the little band of condemned men. There were now fifteen who regularly crowded into the murky, fetid room to sit on dirty straw that covered the cold stone floor and listen to Philip's words of comfort. Lancaster continued to be his strongest support, every day bringing a new prisoner to the group.

But most remarkable of all was Doyle, who had entered spewing curses on that first visit. Following Lancaster's continued witnessing, Doyle had asked forgiveness for his sins and was now a most enthusiastic worker among his fellow prisoners, going from cell to cell, sharing his own clear sense of forgiveness and striving to bring the same to his fellow sufferers.

Today Philip sat on the straw with the condemned men and listened to Doyle preach. "I say to you, it matters not which side of the walls we be on. It is absolutely impossible to be happy, either in time or eternity, without knowing your sins are forgiven ..."

Philip couldn't help thinking what a shame this man was due to be hanged in two days. If he could have received an education, he would have made a fine preacher. His voice, which reverberated so well off the stone walls, could have carried as well in a parish church.

But then as Philip rose and his own voice filled the stone room with prayer, he reflected that the same could be said of himself. He too was preaching in prison when he would sooner be ministering in a church. At the end of his prayer, he looked at the faces around him and had to ask forgiveness that he had complained. For the moment this was his place of ministry, and he would do it to his utmost, with thankfulness to the God who allowed him a place.

He turned to Atkins, a youth of about nineteen. "Are you afraid to die?"

"No, sir. Really, I am not."

"Wherefore are you not afraid?" Philip continued the catechism.

"I have laid my soul at the feet of Jesus; therefore, I am not afraid to die."

Philip continued around the room. Next was Gardner, a journeyman carpenter, about fifty, who gave a strong report of what the Lord had done for his soul. And on down the row, to one Thompason, an illiterate young man who, in spite of a severe speech defect, gave assurance that he too was saved from the fear of death and was perfectly happy in his Savior.

That evening Philip went home knowing that the next night would be his last with those men. Although hardly a humorous situation, he couldn't suppress a small smile at the irony. He had prayed fervently for a congregation he wouldn't have to leave. So he was supplied with a congregation that would be leaving him.

He lit his fireplace, but did not take off his coat. It would be some time yet before the room was comfortably warm, even on a June night. But the flame would be enough to fry a rasher of bacon to accompany his evening tea. Stepping to his cupboard, he saw the letter his landlady had laid on his bed.

At first the name Perronet made his breath come in a strange way; but on second look, he saw that the post was from Vincent, not from his daughter. He lit a candle to supplement the dim light from the window and read. The words brought such a surge of hope to his heart that he jumped to his feet and circled his small room in five strides before making himself read the letter through a second time.

. . . As the Bishop of Ely is an old friend of mine, I have

taken the liberty of writing to him myself to recommend you for this post. I was able to tell him I have personally heard you preach in my own pulpit. Further, with Cambridge in his diocese, he should be well-disposed to your academic credentials.

I wish you well, my Son. May His blessings go with you.

Vincent Perronet

The living at Grantchester was open, and it was in the gift of the Bishop of Ely. That lovely village on the banks of the Cam, just outside Cambridge, was without a vicar. A vicarage—not just a curacy. It was far more than he had dared pray for.

Philip's first impulse was to pack clean linen in his bag and set out at once. He smiled for the second time that evening. Such impulsive behavior was unlike him; besides, he could not leave yet. He had a commitment at the Fleet to fulfill first. He cut two slices of bacon from a slab and placed it in a wire rack to cook over the fire. In spite of the excitement in his heart, this night would be spent the same as every other—alone in his room.

The next night, however, was unlike any other he had experienced. Armed with adequate money for garnishment, Philip convinced the keeper to allow the condemned men to assemble together in one cell so that they might pass their last hours together in prayer. The men came in quietly and sat on the straw and stone. Nothing in their outward appearance showed that they had but a few hours to live. Philip began the gathering by reading from the Prayer Book, first the Commination: "'Now seeing that all are accursed who do err and go astray from the commandments of God, let us (remembering the dreadful judgment hanging over our heads) return unto our Lord God with all contrition and meekness of heart, bewailing and lamenting our sinful life . . .'"

Lancaster led the others with a loud, "Amen."

Then Philip turned to the Psalm: "'Have mercy upon me, O God, after Thy great goodness; according to the multitude of Thy mercies do away mine offenses. Wash me thoroughly from my wickedness; and cleanse me from my sin, for I acknowledge my faults; and my sin is ever before me.'"

And finally the prayer, as those who were sitting shifted to their knees: "'O Lord, we beseech Thee, mercifully hear our prayers, and spare all those who confess their sins unto Thee; that they, whose consciences by sin are accused, by Thy merciful pardon may be absolved; through Christ our Lord. Amen.'"

The men then continued in prayer, some extemporaneously, for it seemed that the Lord had opened their mouths and their hearts. Philip was sure he had never before so truly sensed the reality of God's mercy. Tonight this mercy was ennobling these illiterate, condemned prisoners who so wholeheartedly sought it and so fully accepted it.

All too soon the clanking of the iron door brought with it an announcement of the time. The turnkey barked his orders and led the prisoners into the press yard. But even in the gray of predawn in the stone-walled yard, with the carts that were to transport them to Tyburn parked by the gate, a solemn joy and peace shone on each countenance. Philip took Doyle's hand. "My dear man, how do you find yourself?"

"Find myself! Why truly, sir, my soul is so filled with light, love, and peace that I am the same as if I had naught else within me!" He then turned to the jailers in the yard and began telling them of the love of God to him and his assurance of knowing that God for Christ's sake had forgiven all his sins.

But this was cut short, as the jailers began pushing their charges into the carts. Philip, who had received permission from the warden to accompany the men, was shoved into the first cart with Doyle and Lancaster as roughly as all the rest. Lancaster sat on his own coffin. Doyle, who could not afford one and so would share a pauper's grave, sat on the rough floor of the tumbril.

The horses started off with a jerk, bouncing the heavy wooden cart on its iron wheels over the rough stone pavement. The procession went down Ludgate Hill and turned into Holborn. Already a crowd had gathered along the street. This was a hanging day, and the populace was prepared to enjoy it to the full. Hanging day held the status of a holiday. Throughout the city master coachmakers, tailors, shoemakers—any who must deliver orders within a given time—always bore in mind to observe to their customers, "That will be a hanging day, and my men will not be at work."

Holborn became Oxford Street, and as the carts approached Tyburn Road, the crowds became denser and rowdier.

"Hey, wanta rubber neck, Mate?"

"Swing 'em up 'igh, Charlie, so's they can 'ave a better view!"

"Cooee, they got a parson too! I always knowed they was a thievin' lot!" A tomato squashed through the bars of the cart, and red streaks ran down Philip's sleeve. He suddenly realized that to the observers, he was no different from the prisoners. He felt shame wash over him as he understood that the crowd thought him condemned too.

And then he was ashamed of his shame. Was this not exactly what Christ had suffered for him—to be numbered among the transgressors? And was it not appropriate that he, who but for the mercy of Christ would be condemned eternally for his own sins, should taste just a small portion of what Christ suffered in taking on the sin of others, in identifying with the damned?

The tumbril lurched to a stop. Two carts from Newgate were there ahead of them. A great cheer went up from the crowd as the pealing of church bells, led by those from St. Sepulchre's, announced that the proceedings were to begin. Holidayers passed gin bottles from hand to hand; children clambered atop their parents' shoulders; and the lucky ones with front-row spaces spread picnic baskets on rugs.

And then a louder cheer rose as the first cart opened, and the most popular of the condemned, a well-known highwayman called Daring Dirk, stepped out. Highwaymen held the ancient privilege of heading the procession of malefactors, and he was immediately mobbed by spectators trying to snatch a memorial such as a lock of his hair or a piece of his clothing. With an air of *noblesse oblige* Dirk pulled bits of lace from his sleeve and buttons from his coat and bestowed them upon the throng.

Jack Ketch, as all public executioners were called after a well-known hangman from the previous century, stepped forward as if to greet the highwayman. But in truth, his hand was not held out to shake, rather to receive his agreed payment from his victim. The larger the bribe, the easier the hangman could make the death, even to pulling on the legs of the victim or to sitting across his shoulders to accelerate strangulation. Dangerous Dirk produced a fat wad; he had no intention of suffering long. Then with a jaunty wave he mounted the scaffold. At the top he turned again and tossed his feathered hat into the crowd with a flourish. The story of his gallant death would be told and retold, and his fame as a folk hero was assured.

But in the third tumbril, the mood was not one of such reckless bravado, nor of grim resignation, but rather of quiet rejoicing as Philip led the men in a hymn.

The door of the cart opened. Doyle was the first to stand up. Lifting his eyes to heaven, he said with a loud voice so all around could hear, "Lord, didst not Thou die for sinners? Thou didst die for me!" Turning around to the multitude, he prayed out loud. When he was finished, Philip could not see a dry eye anywhere around him. Then all from the cart went forward together.

Philip paid Jack Ketch. At the top of the stairs Doyle, Lancaster, Gardner, and Thompason turned as one man and cried, "Lord Jesus, receive our spirits!"

10

*C*atherine was sitting with Durial going over the linen cupboard lists and checking the mending needs when Audrey interrupted with a soft knock. "Mr. Ferrar's below askin' for the mistress and Miss Perronet. I told 'im Mr. Ned was still on circuit."

"Will you see him, Catherine? I simply must get this chore finished this afternoon." Durial sighed at the mountain of folded linen beside her.

"Gladly." Catherine was out the door before her word was finished.

But at the bottom of the stairs she halted sharply. "Philip! Are you ill? You look ghastly." She was accustomed to the thinness of his frame and the sharpness of his cheekbones, but the hollowness around his normally bright eyes was alarming. "Audrey, bring a tray of coffee and cold meats to the parlor." She led the way into the sitting room.

"Thank you." Philip folded his long body into a wing-back chair. "I am not ill, but I have had such an experience. . . . I have just watched four dear friends die." And he told her of the execution.

Catherine poured coffee from the silver pot Audrey set

before her on a small table and considered his account. "Do you not rejoice that their souls are now in Heaven?"

"Assuredly I do. I think my grief is more for myself. For them it is a glorious release. I feel bereft. Is that selfish in me?"

If his question had not been so earnest and at such a sad time, she would have laughed. He was the most unselfish creature she had ever met. "On the contrary, Philip. It is your great desire to give of yourself in service that causes you grief. Like a mother when her last child marries, you now have no one left to minister to." And with a flash of insight she understood that he was again, but in a different way, suffering the kind of trauma he had known in the loss of his curacy. Again he had put down roots. Even as shallow as the stone floor of the prison had required those roots to be, the pulling up was painful.

"Philip," she spoke rapidly in her rush to comfort him, "the Lord will provide a new place of service. He has promised. 'He that walketh in a perfect way, he shall serve Me.' I do believe that, Philip. He knows your desire. You shall serve Him."

"Thank you, Catherine. I believe it too. And your hopeful words put me in mind of something I had quite forgotten. I didn't come to mourn with you, but to tell you of the letter I received from your father and to take my leave."

"Leave?"

"Yes, your father has recommended me to the Bishop of Ely for a living that has come open. I shall leave in the morning for an interview. It is just possible—"

"Oh, Philip! It's more than just possible. It's quite certain!" She jumped to her feet. "Philip! What a wonderful answer to prayer! Bishop Gooch is an old friend of Father's. I'm certain he will give you a warm interview."

Philip held up his hand in protest and tried to argue that the matter was by no means certain, but Catherine would not hear of it. She had prayed too long for a place of service for Philip and had reaffirmed her faith in God's guidance too fully to allow any doubt now. They talked at length of the vicarage and of Philip's travel plans.

"And when will you return?" Catherine asked.

"If the weather's fine, Cambridge is only three days' ride, then half a day on to Ely. I should be able to accomplish it in just over a week."

"And will you preach on the way?"

"Oh, of course. I haven't thought this through well. Yes, the Cambridge Society has requested a preacher. I shall hold services in Cambridge, Newmarket, Burwell . . . two weeks at least. Will Ned be back by then?"

"I think not. He and Charl have gone clear to Newcastle. But, Philip, if you are not back by Sunday, you will miss your birthday. I had thought to make you a poppy-seed cake."

"My birthday?"

"Yes, don't you remember at Shoreham when Philothea decreed the second Sunday in Trinity to be your birthday?"

"No, I had entirely forgotten. I shall be sorry to miss the cake."

And that was as personal as his leave-taking was to be—he would miss the cake. The conversation turned briefly back to his prison ministry, with Catherine renewing her vow to aid the Smithson family and Philip telling more of Doyle's conversion. In spite of her serene exterior, however, Catherine was troubled inside. She didn't want to talk only of Philip's work. Did he care for nothing else? No one else? Was his every thought only for those to whom he could minister? As important as his work was, couldn't there be more?

She looked into those steady eyes of his, so revealing and yet so shuttered at the same time. Warm, kind, intelligent eyes that told nothing about the man behind them and made no revelation of his emotions.

The fact that she at least partially understood his isolation didn't always make it easy to accept. There were times, like right now, when she wanted to smash the wall he had erected around himself so that she could get to the real Philip inside.

At times she wondered if, indeed, he had emotions behind that unrevealing face. But she never wondered for long because, attuned to him as she was, she had learned to read the tiny looks and gestures that gave him away. And she never, not even in her most depressed moments, doubted that, once she reached him, the real Philip would be worth finding.

Now the tightness around his mouth and the jerky motion with which he placed his black shallow-brimmed hat on his head told her of the importance he placed on this journey.

"God go with you," she called from the doorway as he mounted Jezreel.

The thought that he was going to interview for a living should have raised Catherine's spirits; but as she turned away from the closed door and crossed the darkened hall, she felt heavyhearted. She searched her mind for a comforting thought and was horrified at the verse that came to her mind: "And Stephen went out and preached the word of God boldly." No! She would not think about that—about the stones, the mad bulls, the drunken threats Philip would face. Nor would she think about what preaching in similar circumstances had cost Stephen. That was in God's hands.

There was only one thing she could do, and that was what she would concentrate on. Right there in the hall she closed her eyes; and forcing frightening images away, she deliberately thought about Philip preaching calmly to the throng, Philip proclaiming God's love and God's Word, Philip placing all his faith in the power of God's protection.

She would pray and continue with her own work. Doing whatever her hand found to do could be a great comfort in times of difficulty. And in Durial's home, there was never any lack of work. Catherine returned to the drawing room to find her sister-in-law hard at work polishing the furniture. "Durial,"

Catherine protested, "Audrey rubbed the tables with lemon oil not a fortnight ago. Can't you rest?"

Durial ran an impatient hand across her forehead. "With Ned forever away on his preaching trips, someone must keep our home from falling to bits around our ears. The furniture should long ago have been revarnished with alkanet root, rose pink, and linseed oil, but when do you think Ned could have time to see to such as that?"

With a ¬igh Catherine picked up a rag and the bottle of lemon oil. Monday she would return to her class and would be certain to call on Elmira Smithson.

A few days later when Catherine kept her resolve, the worsening of the Smithsons' situation made her almost wish she hadn't called on them. "I ast Dick about lettin' Isey go back to yer school like you said—" Elmira's speech was interrupted by a racking cough that made Catherine put her hands to her own chest in sympathy. "Dick won't 'ear none o' it. Knew 'e wouldn't—but was good o' you to offer."

Isaiah had returned to sweeping, and Elmira was doing a careful job of all the laundry she could take in, even if bending over the tubs of water made her cough worse. Catherine spoke what words of comfort she could, placed two wheaten loaves on the bare table, and gave a boiled sweet to little Susanna before she left.

The days dragged slowly, and Catherine was more thankful than ever that she had her faith in God's guidance to cling to. No matter how gray the day or how dismal the prospects around her appeared, Catherine could say with the psalmist, "As for God, His way is perfect. . . . He is a buckler to all those that trust in Him." And then Sally's letter came in the next post.

My Dear Catherine,

How precious my memories of our friendship are to me. What joy to know that one other creature has shared my difficulties and understands my feelings. You will note this letter is sent from Ludlow. I fell ill on the way to Bristol from London, so my dear Charles brought me home to my mother for her excellent nursing while he set about his next preaching tour. My sister Betsy is also a most excellent nurse. Perhaps if I am recovered when Charles returns, he might think me strong enough to set up our own home. Write to me of our friends in London. It is beautiful here in Wales, but I miss news of the Society.

Yr ever-faithful friend,
Sally Wesley

The words that fell between the lines of Sally's careful script were the ones that tore at Catherine's heart. Here she was in good health and had only a brother and dear friend to worry about facing the dangers of a circuit. Sally was ill, longing for her own home, missing and fearing for her new husband. Catherine breathed a prayer for her friend and then determined to avoid going the same road herself. No matter how fond her feelings for Philip, she had no desire to spend her life traveling from one decrepit inn to the next so that a new crowd of ruffians might pitch stones at her husband. Not that Philip had ever given her the least indication he would make such an offer; but if he did, she knew she must refuse him. Of course, if he found success with the Bishop of Ely . . .

Philip's great haste to reach the Bishop caused him to plan only one night for revisiting the familiar sights of Cambridge. He tethered Jezreel in St. Andrew's Street and, for the first time since his graduation five years before, entered the gates of Emmanuel College. Here he had worked and studied for three years as a sizar, acting as servant first to young Lord Leatham and then to Percy Chalmers, noblemen who came to the university to acquire a smattering of classics and mathematics between rounds of parties. Since men of independent means who were not destined for the Church or the Bar weren't hindered by any requirement to take examinations or attend classes, Philip's life had been a constant struggle to please his cavalier masters while maintaining his own academic standards. Examinations were required of one like Philip who came of the servant class and who would take Holy Orders.

Philip recalled the nights of study constantly interrupted by demands that he serve liquor, polish boots, and carry notes to ladies. At first he had had only his own determination to carry him through. But then, after acquaintance with William Law's book led him to understand the basis for a devout and holy life, the service ceased to be a yoke and became instead a challenge which he met gladly.

Now he walked across the wide green court toward the colonnade built by Sir Christopher Wren and entered the chapel behind. Emmanuel College, founded in the sixteenth century by Queen Elizabeth's chancellor of the exchequer, had been built on the site of a Dominican friary which was abandoned during the dissolution of church properties by Henry VIII. From the first the college had had a Puritan bias, ties which were strengthened during Cromwell's reign and which even now Philip could sense in the austere white walls, stone floor, and plain glass windows of the chapel. The only contrast came from the well-proportioned carving in the dark wood furnishings.

Philip left the chapel and walked on beside the herb and rose gardens lining the Elizabethan walls of the court, built largely from the stones of long-crumbled Cambridge Castle. He paused at the doorway of the elegant, unpuritanical Hall and recalled serving his superiors at high table. But for all the nobility who had passed through these doors, the two most famous students had been commoners—William Law and the Puritan cabinet minister, John Harvard, who went to America and founded a college to train clergymen in the colony of Massachusetts.

Philip smiled as he turned away from Hall. His university years, as his orphanage years, had been marked by his detachment from his fellow men. He had not minded wearing his coarse gown, signifying the lowest rank of undergraduate in the scale topped by the elegantly robed noblemen. They had been years of vast mental and spiritual growth, in the sum, not unhappy to look back upon.

Philip had intended only a brief walkabout before he settled into a room at The Sun, but when he reemerged onto St. Andrew's Street, he ran almost bodily into a figure from his past. "Thomas Thornton!" Philip clasped the man's arm as much to steady him from their near collision as in greeting. "Are you still in Cambridge?"

Thornton had been a close friend of Percy Chalmers whom Philip served at Emmanuel. "Went into the family firm of solicitors in Newmarket. See by your garb you took orders. Seems I recall you had Methody tendencies—didn't become a Jacobite or anything crack-brained, did you?" Thornton looked over his shoulder as if he didn't want to be seen in suspect company should the answer be wrong.

"Oh, I assure you I'm anything but a political rebel. Long live King George. I am with the Methodist Society, however."

"Meeting tonight, but I suppose that's what you're here for."

Philip assured him he had no idea what he was talking about.

"Big Methody meeting on Christ's Pieces. Some Welch fellow, Harris, preaching. Thought I'd look in on the doings. Care to come along?"

Philip started to refuse. He'd planned on an early evening and riding on at dawn the next morning. But his conscience smote him. In his intense desire to reach Ely, he had forgotten his stated intentions of holding meetings in the area. Certainly he should go and lend his support to the preacher.

They arrived at the open green field at the end of Emmanuel Street just as the crowd began singing. It was a new experience for Philip to stand at the back of such a gathering. He found the perspective most interesting as he surveyed the farmers and housewives still carrying their baskets of vegetables from the Cambridge market. In spite of a few catcalls, they seemed an unusually peaceable group—until the leader began the third song and complaints began.

"What's a' matter—preacher afraid to speak?"

"Yeah, Parson—cat got yer tongue?"

"What is this 'ere? Some 'oity-toity musical society?"

"We want preachin'!"

And then the rumor spread through the crowd—Howell Harris had not arrived as scheduled. It was certain the local vicar would not under any circumstances preach in an open field. Philip knew what he must do.

"Seems I'll have to take leave of your company." He bowed to Thornton. "They need a preacher, and that's my calling."

He didn't wait for the startled expression to leave his companion's face. "I daresay, field preaching—"

As Philip pushed his way through the throng, he breathed a prayer, "O Lord, show me what to say to these people."

The crowd made way for him, and he met no obstacle until he reached the wooden platform that the Society had dragged onto the grass to make a speaker's platform. In the very front stood a surly young clergyman who would not give way. "My brother, I have come to offer my services as a preacher, but I see you precede me. Perhaps you would like to address this congregation. I should be happy to be numbered among your hearers." Philip made him a bow.

The cleric gave Philip a haughty look and stepped aside just enough to allow him to pass. Relief flooded the distressed song leader's face, and he introduced the preacher newly arrived from London. Philip gave only the briefest thought to the tomatoes and peaches he saw in many market baskets before he announced his topic. He had only his Bible with him, but that was enough to carry him through his favorite sermon on 1 John 5:12, "He that hath the Son hath life; and he that hath not the Son of God hath not life."

The crowd was remarkably well-behaved, and the few tomatoes and dirt clods thrown were poorly aimed. One juicy peach, however, landed squarely on the head of the surly clergyman who was standing so as to block as much of Philip's access to his audience as possible.

Next morning Philip put Cambridge and its memories behind him as he set out for Ely. By midday the path across the flat fenland brought him in sight of the cathedral standing on its island like a lighthouse on a hill. Even at this time of day mists from the surrounding waters rose around the building, emphasizing the fact that it was bordered on all sides by wild and treacherous marsh. A hundred years before, Cromwell had completed the plans begun by Charles I to drain the fens and thereby brought hundreds of square miles of land under the plow. So now Philip rode through fields of flax, wheat, and hay.

For much of the sixteen miles, Philip meditated on his forthcoming interview and prayed that this would be the answer to his waiting. But then Jezreel's hooves clattered over one of the many wooden bridges spanning the drains that crisscrossed the fens, and he saw the eels swimming in the water. His thoughts turned to his surroundings, and he gave a smile for the legend which lent the town its name. These eels and all those populating the streams of East Anglia were believed to be the descendants of the monks of the tenth century who had taken wives and were punished by the reformer St. Dunstan by being turned into eels.

Philip sat even taller than usual in the saddle as he rode past the great cathedral and on to the Bishop's Palace. The bishop's chaplain answered Philip's knock. For a moment Philip couldn't believe what he saw. Just in time he checked his impulse to groan and bestowed an uncertain smile on the man before him. It was the surly cleric from last night's meeting.

"Philip Ferrar. I believe My Lord Bishop is expecting me." Philip offered his letter of introduction from Vincent Perronet.

"Please wait here." The chaplain turned, and Philip noted

that his hair and clothes were scrubbed clean of any traces of the peach. He ushered Philip into a richly appointed gallery presided over by the portrait of a dour-looking bishop in a black velvet cape. In contrast to the luxuriousness of the furnishings, the severe austerity of the attitudes around him chilled Philip. He dared not think what his future held if he met yet another refusal.

The sound of the chaplain's quick step on the polished wooden floor told Philip he wouldn't have long to wait. "His Lordship will see you now." The chaplain's lips curled in a cross between a smirk and a smile, but his eyes were hard.

The bishop sat at his desk, light from the leaded window beside him falling on his white hair. A wave of his ringed hand told Philip to take a seat. The bishop looked at the papers on his desk and went straight to the heart of the matter.

"You seek appointment to the vicarage of Grantchester. Mr. Perronet is most warm in his support. Why did you leave your curacy in Midhurst?"

The unpleasant must be brought into the open sooner or later. Philip was glad to have it be sooner. "I was dismissed for teaching Jesus Christ and Him crucified, My Lord."

The ringed hand waved the statement aside. "And what have you been doing since that time?"

"I have been doing itinerant preaching."

"Ah, yes. I have heard of your unseemly enterprise last night. Grantchester is a quiet, well-behaved parish. I do not believe an enthusiastic vicar would best suit their needs."

The thrust came so rapidly and so quietly that at first Philip was not aware of the pain from its cut.

"I thank you for the courtesy of your call. But do not let me detain you any longer." Dr. Gooch rose and rang a bell. When the chaplain appeared in the doorway, the bishop added, "Mr. Flagg will give you a glass of Madeira on your way out."

Philip rose, made a mechanical bow to the bishop, and left the palace without the support of the offered glass of wine. The complete interview, upon which his entire future hung, had lasted less than five minutes.

As if of their own volition, his feet carried him across the grass to the cathedral. He continued his sleepwalk down the great nave until he stood beneath the glory of the cathedral—one of the wonders of medieval engineering and carpentry—Ely's lantern. Arching his head back, he looked up into the glorious aureola formed from the light shafting downward through the high traceried windows of the octagonal tower. As he looked at the display of pure light that spread from the lantern over the wooden ceiling and throughout the whole church, it seemed that some of that same light touched his soul. Its warmth thawed just a drop of all that was frozen within him. But it was enough to allow the Word of God to speak through his numbness, "Cause me to hear Thy lovingkindness . . . for in Thee do I trust; cause me to know the way wherein I should walk; for I lift up my soul unto Thee."

It seemed he had come to the end of the path. But then he looked up into the light, and his Guide was there to lead him through the uncharted way. In the great cathedral, Philip knelt with the light from the magnificent lantern of the tower shining on him like a benediction. And in his pain, he thought of another who had been denied all he had worked for and hoped for because he did what he believed to be right. Perhaps it was his recent visit to Emmanuel College that brought William Law so strongly to his mind as he prayed. Soon Philip realized he was no longer praying, but instead meditating on Law's life and feeling a great kinship with this man. After achieving the goal for which he had worked and studied—after becoming a Fellow of Emmanuel—Law had it taken from him just five years later when he refused to swear the oath of allegiance to the new line of German kings.

Though a priest of the Church of England, though a man with the highest sense of the responsibilities of the clerical office and the duties of his order, Law gave up all right to conduct a service, to celebrate the Holy Communion, or to preach a sermon. He chose instead to live in seclusion—studying, praying, and guiding souls through his writing and his charities.

As the light from the lantern spread throughout the cathedral along the vaulted arches, so the light of God's leading spread through Philip's heart and mind. He knew what he would do. He rose to his feet with a much lighter spirit. He would go to King's Cliffe. William Law would be his counselor.

It was a long ride the next day on across the fenland and finally through the edge of Rockingham Forest to the tiny village where Law lived. Not until the three symmetrical chimney stacks of the Hall Yard House came into view did Philip doubt his inspiration to make the trip. What if Law weren't at home? What if he were home, but had no inclination to receive an intruder? What if . . .

Jezreel drew up before the comfortable house built of the local freestone, roofed with greenish slates, and announced their arrival with a whinny. The noise attracted the attention of a black-suited, stout man with broad shoulders and round face who was escorting a bent, ragged man carrying a clean shirt and basket of fresh vegetables across the courtyard. "I shall see you again, my dear friend. Meditate on the words of our Lord." The merry-countenanced man held the gate for the beggar and then turned to Philip, who dismounted with some chagrin at coming so abruptly into the presence of the esteemed William Law.

Philip introduced himself, but found it impossible to explain the purpose of his visit, since he didn't understand it himself. Law, however, seemed to find nothing in the least unusual about having a caller he had not seen for more than five years arrive at his gate in search of counsel and comfort.

"Come in, come in. You have had a long ride? I believe our distribution of food and raiment is done for the day. If any other comes, one of my house can see to it. You have come from London? You must stop here for a time. We get so little word from the great city."

He led the way through the courtyard and into an old wain-scotted hall. "My study is upstairs." He waved his hand at an ascending staircase. "But let us go through here first; I should like you to meet my companions." The parlor was unoccupied, so Law went through the back door and into the garden. "Ah, we've found you at last," he called to two women sitting on a garden bench. "Mr. Ferrar, Mrs. Hutcheson and Miss Gibbon, my companions and spiritual pupils."

The ladies put aside their books and came forward to welcome Philip, and in a moment he was being given as complete a tour of Law's property as if he were expected to take up residence there. ". . . and on the other side of the paddock," pretty, lace-capped Miss Gibbon said, "is the footbridge over Willow Brook. Beyond that are the schools and almshouses which Mr. Law and Mrs. Hutcheson erected and endowed."

"We now have fourteen girls receiving instruction and clothing in our school," the small, plump Mrs. Hutcheson added.

"And there is my oak tree." Miss Gibbon pointed to a small green sprout. "I planted that when I came to reside here—1744 that was, so it's just an infant yet, but someday it will shade the paddock."

Law's gray eyes and ruddy complexion glowed as he looked at the field washed in the golden light of evening. "It is my habit to take an hour's walk in my fields before supper. Would you care to join me?"

Philip begged time to stable Jezreel and then joined his host with pleasure. They walked along a footpath bordered on one side with a field of waist-high dark green grain and on the other with a brambled hedgerow, lush with ripe berries and vibrant with birdsong. "My favorite form of vesper," Law said, after they had walked for some time with the birds' arias as the only accompaniment to the rustle of their footsteps in the long grass. "You have sought me out for counsel?"

And suddenly Philip found it so easy, so natural to talk to

this man. He told briefly of his curacy and rejection and now of his work with the Methodist Society. But through all his words rang clearly his desire for a call from God to a place of ministry—a settled, peaceful place to shepherd a flock. And he told of his latest refusal by the bishop.

"And would you have acted differently in Cambridge had you foreseen the results?" Law asked.

"Fifteen souls sought the Savior that night. I could do no other, so help me God."

Law nodded, and his open, agreeable countenance took on an expression of nostalgia. "Relinquishing my college Fellowship for conscience' sake was a melancholy affair, but had I done what was required of me to avoid it, I should have thought my condition much worse. The benefits of my education seemed at an end, but yet the same education had been more miserably lost, had I not learned to fear something more than misfortunes.

"If I were not happier now for that earlier trial, I am persuaded it would be my own fault. Had I brought myself into troubles by my own folly, they would have been very trying; but, I thank God, I can think of them without dejection."

A smile broke across his face. "I recall writing something of the like to my brother George shortly after the occurrence. I remember that my most pressing concern was for my mother. I feared she would be overcome in her concern for me. But the Lord was faithful to sustain those dear to me also."

The bell ringers of King's Cliffe Church began their ancient custom of pealing the hours of the day as the two men turned their steps back toward Law's house.

"It has always been so. I have found the Lord ever faithful. As we are faithful in our devotion to Him, He supplies our need for others to minister to. That is the key to happiness, meeting the needs of others."

When they returned to the house, Law ushered Philip into a long, low-ceilinged dining room where the table stood by a bow window looking onto the garden. Supper was the simplest meal imaginable, consisting of a few biscuits, cheese, and wine. The household servants then joined Law, his guest, and the women for evening prayer and Law's reading of Scripture before everyone retired at nine o'clock.

Alone in his room with only the light of the moon shining through his window, Philip thought of the light that had shined on him at Ely and led him to this house, to this counselor. He was reminded of the Scripture that spoke of coming out of darkness into God's marvelous light. He felt assured that William Law would be instrumental in shedding God's light in his life. Perhaps the first spark had been struck. He thought back over their evening stroll in the fields and recalled Law's words of the importance of filling others' needs with oneself. Thinking on this, Philip felt light and warmth and comfort sink into his soul. He had been so very much alone all his life—isolated in a crowded orphanage. He saw in his own mind the child he had been—the repressed, quiet, good little boy. And he saw the man that little boy had become—quiet, withdrawn, alone, not opening himself to anyone nor allowing anyone close enough to reach his needs.

Catherine was the nearest he had admitted anyone. But the thought of allowing her to come closer and then abandon him was too painful to be borne. However, here in the Hall Yard House he had found sanctuary.

And the peace of King's Cliffe, the peace William Law practiced with his fellow men and before his God, permeated Philip's soul in the following days. Philip had long known peace in solitude, in the ability to withdraw and be comfortable with himself and with God. But this was a new kind of peace Law practiced, as he lived his devout and holy life in a complete giving of himself.

Law rose early and breakfasted in his room on a cup of chocolate before appearing in the drawing room to lead family prayers at nine o'clock. He would then invite Philip to join him in his bedroom upstairs where the morning light fell through the stone-mullioned windows of the bedroom and adjoining study. And throughout the day, William Law put aside his studying and writing to interview each applicant for relief who came to the garden door.

On his third morning there, Philip sat before the fireplace in Law's oak-beamed bedroom while Law interviewed the fourth suppliant of the day in the tiny study that he called his "closet." Philip looked at the hearthstone of the fireplace and noted the hollows Law had worn in places by rubbing his cold feet upon the warm stones. Then he turned to gaze out the windows; through the trees he could just glimpse the school's library and also the almshouses endowed by his host. From the next room he heard Law's counsel to the beggar. "My good man, I shall be happy to meet your needs for half a crown, but see that you spend it wisely. And be assured that I shall do the same. Just as I would not give a poor man money to go see a puppet show, neither would I allow myself to spend it in the same manner. It is a folly and a crime in a poor man to waste what is given him in foolish trifles whilst he wants meat, drink, and clothes. And it would be no less folly or a less crime in me to spend that money in silly diversions which might be so much better spent in imitation of the divine goodness and works of kindness and charity."

Law rose and took the pauper's hand. "And so, my brother, let us both go forth to serve God and man in the doing of good. And remember the words of the Holy Scriptures, 'Blessed be the man that provideth for the sick and needy: the Lord shall deliver him in the time of trouble.' Go now and give as it has been given unto you.

"Miss Gibbon will supply you with a loaf fresh from her oven on your way out." Law stepped to the clothespress in his bedroom and drew out a coarse linen shirt that looked little-worn. "And take this in remembrance of Him who said, 'When one asks for your cloak, give him your coat also.'" Law rang a bell, and a servant appeared to show the man out. Then Law sat in the chair across from Philip.

"You interview every petitioner personally?" Philip asked.

"Certainly. It is only by making our labor a gift and service to the poor that our ordinary work is changed into a holy service and made acceptable to God as our devotion. As charity is the greatest of all virtues, so nothing can make it more amiable in the sight of God than adding one's own labor to it."

Philip shook his head. "And for such as this they call you an enthusiast?"

Law gave his familiar guffaw of laughter. "I believe the term is 'a celebrated enthusiast,' the very worst kind—one who not only teaches the way of salvation, but lives it as well."

In an uncharacteristic show of emotion, Philip hit the arm of his chair. "But that's monstrous. To call a man an enthusiast is to call him a leper—a man to be carefully shunned." A note of bitterness attended his words.

"My two housemates and I strive to live our lives based on a literal application of the principles of the Sermon on the Mount, so I guess it is appropriate that some should say all manner of evil against us for righteousness' sake. We attempt to rejoice and be glad in it. But I do not live like a nonjuror. I delight in attending every service of my parish church." Just then the bells pealed the hour from their Norman tower across the field. "And at my special request the rector always has the Psalms sung. I have always been a high churchman. Through my study and writing, I wish to dispel the prevalent notion that piety is generally accompanied by intellectual weakness."

"*A Serious Call* has done much to dispel that notion."

"The Lord's leading is a great and marvelous thing. I often wonder if I would have written it if I had retained my Fellowship. I left Emmanuel and went as tutor to Mr. Edward Gibbon, brother of my excellent companion. By the by, my old student now has a son of his own who is showing a precocious interest in Roman history. Shouldn't be surprised if the young scamp might make a name for himself someday. At any rate, the following year I accompanied young Edward to Emmanuel as his governor and wrote the book while there. The Lord has seen fit to bless it in His work."

"Its detractors have said it sets impossibly high standards—that it is not practicable. But I see that you indeed practice it thoroughly."

"Indeed, the standard is high. But we shall do well to aim at the highest degree of perfection if we may thereby at least attain to mediocrity."

A knock at the door interrupted their discussion. A shabbily dressed woman stood there seeking charity. After a short interview, Law gave her a pail of milk from the four cows he kept and sent a large kettle of soup to her hungry children. But the soup was not ladled from the pot over the kitchen fire until Law tasted it first himself. After a careful sip of the steaming liquid, he went to the garden door and called, "Miss Gibbon, are there any more leeks in the garden? The broth is a bit weak today."

The additional vegetables strengthened the soup, and the woman went home to feed her children.

"Do you ever turn any away?" Philip asked.

Law gave his ready, cheerful laugh. "If a rogue came for money, even if I knew him to be a rogue, I would give him money, hoping for the best and believing it my duty to give to all who might be in need. It may be that I often give to those who do not deserve it or who will make ill use of my alms, but what then? Is this not the very method of divine goodness? Does not God make His sun to rise on the evil and on the good? Shall I withhold a little money or food from my fellow creature for fear he should not be good enough to receive it of me? Don't I beg of God to deal with me not according to my merit, but according to His own great goodness? And shall I be so absurd to withhold my charity from a poor brother because he may perhaps not deserve it? Shall I use a mirror toward him, which I pray God never to use toward me?"

It was now tea time, but Law, as was his custom, did not join his companions at the tea table. He chose rather to eat a few raisins, standing while they sat. As at all meals, the food was served on wooden platters. Not, Law explained, from any notion about unnecessary luxury, but because it appeared to him that a china plate spoiled the knives.

The days at King's Cliffe would forever remain in Philip's mind as a foretaste of Heaven, with William Law coming the closest he had ever known to an earthly father. But at last the time came when he must leave. On Philip's last night in Hall Yard House, Law hosted a musical gathering. This was Law's most pleasurable recreation, and he had constructed a handsome wainscotted room with a high-coved ceiling, elegantly decorated with festoons of plasterwork, where Miss Gibbon played works of Bach on the organ.

The next day, beginning his long ride back to London, Philip looped Jezreel's reins over the saddle, drew Law's book from his saddlebag, and read again a favorite passage.

> All worldly attainments, whether of greatness, wisdom, or bravery, are but empty sounds; and there is nothing wise, or great, or noble, in any human spirit, but rightly to know and heartily worship and adore the great God. That is the support and life of all spirits, whether in Heaven or on earth.

He put the book away and thought of the way ahead. Now, after this time of spiritual refreshment, he must return to the real world, to live these principles in the place God had for him. As he guided Jezreel down the road, he thought of the map he sought for his life—looked at his past and thought of the future.

And he could not think of the future without thinking of Catherine. His time with Law had taught him the importance of giving of himself. For the first time in his carefully detached existence, Philip was aware of the possibility, perhaps even the necessity, of filling another person's need with himself—his presence and his personality. It was a totally new concept for him. As he had long ago determined that he didn't need anyone, it had never occurred to him that the reverse might be true—that someone could need him, and not just his preaching.

He was trained and experienced in meeting others' needs with Jesus Christ—with introducing them to Jesus as a person—but the idea of filling a need by presenting himself left him shaken.

But, of course, that was ridiculous. Catherine had turned to him as a friend in her disappointment over Charles Wesley, had leaned on him for support in the darkness of the Fleet, had shared her concerns with him for the safety of her brother, but Catherine didn't really *need* him. She had a large family she could turn to; the Society had the deepest respect for her and all the Perronets . . . anyone would help Catherine. Why would she need him? But then why had she turned to him?

And what could he offer her? All the new spiritual insights he had gained from William Law did not change the realities one jot. He was still a foundling receiving only a meager stipend from the Society for his preaching, and he had no prospects of ever securing a settled living.

And Catherine would be the first person he must tell of his rejection when he reached London in five days' time. When he thought of the disappointment he would see in her eyes, he shrank from the task.

He couldn't go back; he couldn't tell Catherine. He had failed, had been rejected again. Even the recommendation of Vincent Perronet hadn't been enough. He had hoped so to have this to offer her. Now he would never be able to speak what was in his heart. He would be forever alone.

*I*n spite of her outward composure, Catherine was experiencing inner panic. Ned had returned from his circuit ride with Charl, bringing reports of unrest and division among the Methodist preachers in the north. . . . Sally Wesley was expecting a baby, and she and Charles had taken a house in Bristol—good news except that this would mean he would be severely reducing his itinerant ministry, a move causing concern for the work and back-biting gossip among Society members divided in their support of the Wesley brothers. People now openly talked of the rift between John Wesley and George Whitefield, and there were rumors of a split between Charles and John. . . . Elmira Smithson's cough sounded worse each time Catherine visited, and there seemed no possibility of freeing her husband from debtors' prison. . . . Durial's sharp tongue was more caustic than ever as she hectored her husband for a settled lifestyle, to give up circuit-riding and spend more time at home with her.

The list went on, but the fact that almost overwhelmed Catherine was Philip's continued absence. He was never out of her mind, and she hated to admit how much she missed him.

When she looked in her own mirror, she hardly recognized the strained, white face and the round, dark eyes with their hollow look of bereavement. She prayed silently, *I do believe You will take care of all this, Lord. But when?*

On Thursday she returned from the Foundery feeling more wilted than usual. Her students had shown more propensity to wiggle and giggle than to read, and the late summer combination of high heat and higher humidity made the mere thought of labor exhausting. Yet Durial persisted with her housekeeping schedule. With a sigh, Catherine donned a large white apron and joined the entire household staff in the kitchen to help with the preserving.

"There is a peck of plums in the garden that needs pitting," Durial said. "We shall be glad of my special damson jelly this winter."

Catherine pulled a bentwood chair into the shade and began her sticky task. But the peck was less than a quarter done when she heard a horse's hooves on the gravel. The pale blond head she saw above the hedge made her forget the heat and the plum stains on her hands and apron.

"Philip! You've been gone so long." As on that spring day in the woods, she ran toward him, and even more fiercely than then she longed for him to open his arms to receive her.

But his bleak face stopped her. "Philip . . ." It was as if she had run into a wall. Tears threatened to brim in her eyes, but she looked quickly away. If only he would open up to her—could open up. "You've had a long ride. Would you care to walk in the garden?"

They walked where they had before, but the glory was gone. Even his long-awaited presence beside her brought no comfort. The set of his shoulders and the jerky motion of his hands told her his news was bad.

He hesitated, and she knew he wanted to break the news to her gently. But there was no gentle way. "I was refused."

The thin line of his sensitive mouth told her how much he hated saying those words; no matter how calmly he spoke, they had come at great cost. The very briefness of the statement was as final as a locked gate. And it cost her to respond in a likewise unemotional manner, to honor his reticence. For a moment she could not speak. Then, "I shall tell Audrey to prepare some lemonade."

They sat in the shade and sipped cool drinks, but inside, Catherine was seething. Her world had crumbled. This was far worse than the news of Charles Wesley's marriage had been because she cared far more deeply for Philip. And now even if her inklings that Philip returned her regard had any foundation in truth, she had no hope for a future with him. A few nights ago in a dream, she had viewed herself through the eyes of another. She had been at Shoreham, kneeling in the garden, wearing a blue dress, and holding an infant in her arms. She rose and walked toward the person watching her, cuddling the precious bundle to her breast. When she woke, she knew that she had been walking to Philip, carrying their child. But now it could not be.

"Would you care for more lemonade?" The words were a mockery, but she must say something.

Before Philip could answer, a clatter of hooves and flying gravel called them to the front drive. They arrived just as Ned rushed out the front door and Charles Wesley flung off his sweating horse. "My brother intends to ruin himself!" Wesley began his story even as Ned led the way into the parlor.

"You must help me. This insanity must be stopped." Charles drew a crumpled letter from his pocket and handed it to Ned. "He didn't even write to me personally—just sent a copy of a letter to a third person. He intends to marry Grace Murray."

Catherine had never seen the soft-spoken Charles so agitated. He strode around the room spouting disconnected sentences. "The scandal will be unthinkable. It will bring to an end everything we have labored for. She has been promised to John Bennett for months. And now she accepts my brother too! In the past she has suffered serious mental illness, and I have grave concerns for her balance now." He threw his hands into the air.

"It is unthinkable. You must help me. There's no one else I can turn to. This calamity must be stopped."

"Of course, we will help you." Ned clasped his friend's shoulders. "What would you have us do?"

"Ride with me. We must go to Newcastle now."

Catherine's heart sank, thinking of the three-hundred-mile ride. "Philip, you've just returned from a journey and have not even had a good meal yet." As always, his thinness caught at her heart.

"Durial will set a table for us, and I can supply you with clean linen." Ned flung her objections aside. Within a short time the three men departed. In spite of the lateness of the hour, they were determined not to delay. Catherine felt more alone than ever. She was left with the drudgery of her duty and the difficulty of the situations around her; but worse, the one shining hope she had held to for the future had been extinguished. No light shone at the end of the tunnel.

In the month that Ned and Philip were gone, one island of brightness arose. Catherine's sister Elizabeth, who had been laboring so diligently at the Foundery that Catherine had hardly seen her all summer, announced her engagement to William Briggs, John Wesley's secretary.

"Oh, Elizabeth, I am so happy for you." Catherine hugged her sister and then embraced the smiling bridegroom-to-be. "What a perfect couple you will make. I can't fathom why I hadn't thought of the match myself. You'll go to Shoreham to be married by Papa?"

The couple planned to be off the next day so the banns could be published that very Sunday. And then, though happy for her sister, Catherine felt her desolation even more sharply. "When will it be my turn, Lord? In Your perfect timing, do You have a time for me?" As in answer, she thought of words from Ecclesiastes: "To everything there is a season, and a time to every purpose under the heaven. . . . A time to weep, and a time to laugh; a time to mourn, and a time to dance; . . . a time to embrace, and a time to refrain from embracing; . . . He hath made every thing beautiful in His time: also He hath set the world in their heart, so that no man can find out the work that God maketh from the beginning to the end."

No one can find out the work that God maketh? Then she would have to continue groping her way one step at a time, but with continued faith in her Guide and in His timing.

One thing Catherine refused to give up on was her determination to help the Smithson family. So next Monday when school was dismissed, she took her courage in hand, made sure she had adequate bribe money in her pocket, and hired a carriage to take her to the Fleet. She alighted on the walk outside the huge gray walls that concealed the horror, brutality, disease, and death she knew to be inside. The last time she had stormed these walls, Philip was beside her. Now he was on his way to the north of England, and she was alone. No, she reminded herself, never truly alone. "For Thou art with me, Thy rod and Thy staff, they comfort me."

Just as Sarah Peters had taught her to do, Catherine ignored the stares of sightseers who gathered daily outside the massive entrance gates to watch and wait and steep themselves in the malevolent atmosphere of the gaol. And she ignored as well the jeers of those who thought she was the wife or sister of a prisoner.

"Got a file under your skirts, 'ave ye?" a watcher called.

"Another Edgeworth Bess a' goin' out the window down bed sheets with yer Jack Sheppard, 'eh?"

The rabble roared in delight at this reference to Newgate's most notorious escapee who had made daring breaks to freedom on three occasions with the aid of female friends.

The clanking of the heavy doors cut Catherine off from further taunts. The turnkey took her to Dick Smithson's cell, which seemed to Catherine to be even darker and more crowded than before. Smithson sat in almost exactly the same spot, undoubtedly on the same patch of filthy straw where she had seen him months before. He looked at her with hollow eyes. "What're you doin' 'ere?"

"I'm Catherine Perronet. I was here with Elmira last summer. I used to be Isaiah's teacher."

He nodded slowly, and Catherine felt a surge of hope as she realized that he was not drunk. He had probably run out of money to purchase gin. "I 'member. You was with the tall tow-headed feller that kept comin' back to sing 'ymns with those fellas they 'anged."

"Yes." She sorely wished for Philip's company today.

"Must be somethin' to a religion that makes men sing the night afore they go to Tyburn. And that would bring a fella like that one 'ere just to sing with 'em. I 'eard tell 'e rode in the death cart to the gallows with Lancaster and Doyle."

"News travels in here."

"Ain't nothin' else to do." He shrugged.

"And do you know that Elmira is sick? Her cough is worse every time I see her."

Even in the gloom of the cell Smithson's eyes showed his fear at the hopelessness of his situation. "I know. Don't know what'll become of the young'uns if she takes poorly."

"Mr. Smithson, would you reconsider my proposal to allow Isaiah to return to school?"

"Might do."

"Would you like me to pray with you, like Mr. Ferrar did with Lancaster and the others?"

But the curl of his lip and the set of his jaw told her she had gone too far. The turnkey returned to escort her out. "Mr. Smithson, think about Isaiah. If he could read and write, he could get a good job as a clerk. I'll return in a few days for your answer."

Before leaving she arranged with the warden to rent a pillow and blanket for Dick Smithson and to have a loaf of bread delivered to him from the jail's bakehouse. And she left an equal amount of garnish for the jailer as well to be certain her instructions were carried out.

At first Catherine felt considerable hope as she looked forward to Smithson's decision. But when, on her promised return a few days later, she found him far gone with gin and unwilling to hear more of her proposal, her heart sank.

And at home Durial's news was no better. A letter from Ned told them that the men had arrived at Grace Murray's orphan house and hostel in Newcastle where Charles had burst in at eleven o'clock in the morning and cried, "Grace Murray, you have broken my heart!" The letter followed with a tangled account of Charles rushing Grace off to Leeds where she was to meet both men she had promised to marry—John Wesley and John Bennett—then of their return to Newcastle where Bennett awaited without having seen Wesley.

But the part of the account that worried Catherine most was Ned's report that the affair had produced mass unrest and dissension among the Society in Newcastle. "All in the house were filled with anger and confusion; some threatened to leave the house and preach no more with Mr. Wesley." Catherine foresaw dark days ahead for the Methodists who faced enough opposition from outside, without dissension in their own ranks.

That night she went to her room in a cloud of despair. A quick glance at the books on her shelf told her what she wanted to read. Taking her well-worn copy of *Pilgrim's Progress* to a lighted candle by her bed, she turned to the scene of Christian and Hopeful's imprisonment in Doubting Castle, for certainly she felt as much a prisoner of the Giant Despair as Dick Smithson was of his jailer in the Fleet. She read through the scene of Despair exhibiting the bones of doubting pilgrims he had torn limb from limb and thrown into the courtyard, threatening to do the same to his captives in a few days. But later, after Christian and Hopeful prayed, Christian said:

> "What a fool am I to lie in a stinking dungeon, when I may as well walk at liberty! I have a key in my bosom called

DONNA FLETCHER CROW

Promise, that will, I am persuaded, open any lock in Doubting Castle. . . ."

Then Christian pulled it out of his bosom and began to try at the dungeon door, whose bolt, as he turned the key, gave back, and the door flew open with ease, and Christian and Hopeful both came out.

And Catherine knew that she too held the answer to the despair that threatened to imprison her—a key called Promise. She turned the pages of her Bible. "As for God, his way is perfect . . . He is a buckler to all those that trust in him. . . . It is God that girdeth me with strength, and maketh my way perfect. Commit thy way unto the Lord: Trust also in him, and he shall bring it to pass. . . . Wait on the Lord, and keep his way, and he shall exalt thee to inherit the land."

Catherine snuffed her candle and slept better than she had for weeks.

The next week when she drew up before the Foundery and found a freshly combed and scrubbed Isaiah Smithson awaiting her, she knew just how Christian felt when he was back again on the King's Highway.

"Isaiah! Your father said you could come to school again?"

"Yup. Da' said you cared enough to sit on the dirty straw with 'im and then rent 'im a blanket, so 'e figured you was a right 'un."

Catherine shuddered at the degeneration in her pupil's speech. "Isaiah, the class is now several months ahead of you. You shall have to work very hard."

"I brung m' book." He held out the primer she had given him. It was dog-eared and dirty, but it would serve.

A fortnight later when Ned and Philip returned, however, Catherine found that the key of Promise had not yet unlocked the door to solving the Society's problems. The marriage that Charles Wesley felt would be so disastrous for his brother had been averted, but at what cost?

Ned, Durial, Catherine, and Philip sat before the parlor fire on an early October evening as Ned recounted the events of their trip. He spoke slowly and dramatically, relaying the tension of the events that had resulted in the marriage of Grace Murray to John Bennett. The incident had caused a grievous rift between the Wesley brothers and a tidal wave of dissension throughout the Society.

"We pushed straight through to Yorkshire. Charles found George Whitefield preaching to the Societies there and enlisted his help. Whitefield at first counseled that Grace's betrothal to Wesley superseded her promise to Bennett. But in the end Charles's arguments prevailed, and Whitefield acted as Charles's assistant at the wedding of Grace to Bennett."

"Oh, no," Catherine said. "That is sure to drive the wedge between Whitefield and John Wesley deeper yet."

"No." Ned shook his head. "That is the one bright note to this affair. John Wesley joined them in Yorkshire two days after the wedding. He had ridden under great strain for almost forty-eight hours and was too exhausted even to take a room of his own. He lay down beside Whitefield on his bed. It was Whitefield's lot to inform John of the marriage of his intended. In Whitefield's anxiety to console his old friend, he actually wept. Wesley remained dry-eyed, but he was so touched with Whitefield's concern for him that he reestablished fellowship with Whitefield. The rift between them came from a misunderstanding due to being separated by such a great distance. When they were together again, the bond reformed."

"So even though John Wesley lost a wife, he regained a friend," Catherine mused. "And how does Charles view his handiwork in preventing his brother's marriage?"

"Charles is certain he has saved his brother from a great mistake and their life work from shipwreck."

"And John?"

"Reportedly he has not spoken to Charles since the incident."

"Oh, Ned, what will happen to the Societies if there is a rift between the brothers? I continue to hear whispers at the Foundery about disagreements over standards for preachers and of movements to separate—as Charl told us. It frightens me. Where will it end?"

Ned made no reply, so Philip spoke. "It's hard to say. I have always stood firm against separation, and yet it is a possibility I've considered lately. If I were to sign the Acts of Toleration, I could fill a pulpit in a dissenting chapel."

"But, Philip, to leave the Church of England—" Memories of her visit to Canterbury Cathedral and all it meant to her rose in Catherine's mind. To leave the Church of England seemed as unthinkable as to leave England itself.

Philip nodded. "I know. I feel the same way. And any time I consider it, I think of William Law. Even though forced into the position, he refuses to live like a nonjuror; though not allowed to minister in his parish church, he never misses a service. Miss Gibbon told me the rector has preached against Law in his presence; and yet Law continues to sit in the midst of the congregation, saying his prayers and listening to the Bible readings. With his example before me, could I voluntarily dissent?"

The question hung in the air, unanswered. But a few days later something unexpected happened. First, Ned received a letter from Charles Wesley with good news.

> I snatch a few moments before the people come to tell you what you will rejoice to know—that the Lord is reviving His Church; and that George Whitefield and my brother and I are one, a threefold cord which shall no more be broken. My dear friends, you shall have the full account not many days hence, if the Lord bless my coming in, as He has blessed my going out.

The news that the crisis had passed brought great rejoicing at the Foundery; the next week George Whitefield came to

London to give a firsthand account. After the Wednesday preaching service, Whitefield, Ned, Catherine, and Philip gathered in the apartments the Society maintained for visiting evangelists.

"Edward, let me hear this new hymn of yours that seems to be on everybody's lips since I've returned from America. I should like to hear it sung by the man who wrote it."

An organist friend had composed a majestic melody that suited the words perfectly. Ned stood and sang the first three verses of his hymn, and Catherine and Philip joined him on the last verse: "Oh, that with yonder sacred throng / We at His feet may fall! / We'll join the everlasting song, / And crown Him Lord of all."

"Well, Edward, your place in history is secure. I look forward to our singing that around the throne together in Heaven." In spite of his constant squint, which gave his face the impression of a frown, Whitefield's eyes sparkled with pleasure.

"I look forward to singing with you anytime," Ned replied. "And now tell us of the reconciliation you effected between the brothers Wesley."

"I did nothing; the Spirit of our Lord and the love the brothers hold for each other did all. John was with me when Charles arrived at the inn outside Newcastle. At first, he refused to see one he considered to be a Judas. Charles, on his side, declared he would renounce all conversations with his brother except what he would have with a heathen or publican. I simply ignored such inflated stubbornness and constrained the brothers to meet each other."

Whitefield's narrative was interrupted by a servant bringing in dishes of tea. Catherine poured for the company and then urged Whitefield to continue.

"Both brothers were wound up to the highest pitch of emotion and were almost beyond speech, but when they faced each other, the tension snapped and they fell on each other's neck."

"And so the Society is safe?" Catherine asked.

"I pray it will be. But the hardest task still remains—to prove to the Methodists that the work of God is not to be interrupted by any private dissension. And also that though the companionship and love of Grace Murray has been transferred from leader to disciple, the bereavement has left no lasting bitterness behind."

"Can that be done, do you think?"

Whitefield took a deep drink of tea before answering. "In time, pray God." After another pause, made to seem longer by the flickering of candle flame caught in a draught, Whitefield spoke again. "There is much concern of a 'general deadness' in the Society. I have felt it in London in a few persons who are eager to make mischief. Charles says the same is true in Bristol where he feels almost universal coldness, heaviness, and deadness among the people. They have lost near to a hundred members there alone."

"What the people need," Ned suggested, "is something to shake them up."

Whitefield's next words did exactly that to the company in the room. "I am concerned about the work here, but my heart is most truly with my work in America. I must return there soon. I dare to believe that my preaching might help create one nation from those thirteen scattered colonies—unite them under God with each other and with the mother country. I envision the mighty Atlantic Ocean becoming a highway of exchange for gospel preachers.

"Philip," he asked, turning to their silent companion, "will you go with me to help in this work?"

$\mathcal{A}$s winter closed in, bringing with it shorter, darker days and cold winds blowing off the frozen Thames, Philip wrestled with Whitefield's offer. Could he go on without a parish, without his country, without family? Must he forever be alone?

He spent Christmas Eve alone in his room in spite of repeated invitations to come to supper at the Perronets after service at the Foundery. He must reach a decision soon. If he was to go, he must prepare; and if not, Whitefield must be told so he could seek another companion. And whatever he decided, Catherine must be told.

The thought seemed so counter to the new determination he had brought back from King's Cliffe. In the turmoil over Grace Murray, and now as he considered Whitefield's offer, he had made no move to embark on his brave resolve to open himself to Catherine. Indeed, she too seemed more withdrawn than before. For a moment he longed for the days of easy companionship they had shared on their circuit ride.

But before he could decide anything about Catherine, he must know what God desired of him. He picked up his Bible and turned to the Psalms, his heart praying, as David had, for God's guidance: "Show me Thy ways, O Lord; teach me Thy paths . . .

lead me in Thy truth, and teach me; for Thou art the God of my salvation, on Thee do I wait all the day . . . teach me Thy way, O Lord, and lead me in a plain path . . . for Thou art my rock and my fortress; therefore, for Thy name's sake lead me and guide me."

And then he turned to the New Testament where Paul addressed the believers: "For this cause we also, since the day we heard it, do not cease to pray for you, and to desire that ye might be filled with the knowledge of His will in all wisdom and spiritual understanding."

Philip desired with all his heart to know God's will. But as he meditated, a fear gripped him. Had he somehow, somewhere, missed God's will for his life? Could that be the source of his conflict now? "My God, please don't let me be out of Your will." His heart's cry was desperate.

As he continued in God's presence, he felt his prayer answered with a sense of peace and release; and he remembered that the Christian's first responsibility in knowing God's will is being willing to do it. With that thought came the confidence that because he was willing, God would not allow him to miss His divine will. When William Law had told him this, he had not realized its immense implications. If he believed God capable of guiding, he must also believe Him capable of making His will known. The key was seeking God in prayer. And then waiting for the answer to be revealed in His perfect time.

A heavy snow fell on London, choking the streets and making travel from Greenwich to Moorfields slow and hazardous, so Philip did not see any of the Perronets for several days. But on New Year's Eve when the Society held its traditional watch night service at the Foundery, the entire Greenwich household attended. And Philip made no attempt to deny his joy in seeing Catherine standing tall and serene and lovely.

Perhaps because so many had been isolated by the recent storms, there seemed to be a special unity among those who filled the chapel to sing, pray, and worship God as the year 1750 began. At midnight John Wesley served them Communion. Kneeling at the altar with the others, Philip felt a special awareness of God's presence. It was certain to be a momentous year for the Societies and perhaps for himself also. Knowing that he must soon make a decision, he found great comfort in the words of the closing prayer:

> Almighty God, who hast promised to hear the petitions of them that ask in Thy Son's Name, we beseech Thee mercifully to incline Thine ears to us that have made now our prayers and supplications unto Thee; And grant that those things which we have faithfully asked according to Thy will may effectually be obtained . . . to the setting forth of Thy glory, through Jesus Christ our Lord, amen.

And then they stood and sang the song with which all Methodist watch nights concluded: "Hearken to the solemn voice, / The awful midnight cry! / Waiting souls, rejoice, rejoice, / And feel the Bridegroom nigh."

With only a parting bow to his friends, Philip went out into the night of the new year, his confidence in God newly reaffirmed. Whatever the year held, Philip had courage to face it.

Catherine's patience in awaiting God's timing was tested as the January snows drifted into February, and still there were no answers. She sensed Philip's difficulty in responding to George Whitefield's offer. And she knew her hopes for a future with Philip could bear no fruit until that question was settled.

Only once had her brother broached the subject to her. "Cath, I was thinking of the offer Mr. Whitefield extended to Philip. If he should decide to go—that is—I understand the orphan house in Georgia is in need of teachers. Had you ever thought—"

"A teacher of red Indians? Are you weary of my company?" Though she sought to make her answer light, his question continued to plague her. Her head told her that the discomforts and trials of a circuit ride would be as nothing compared to what must be faced by a missionary to the new world. But no matter how sternly her head lectured her heart, her heart would not listen.

And so she lived from day to day, anxious to hear from Philip, and yet reluctant to know his answer.

That Thursday she awoke uncommonly early and lay for a moment, wondering what had disturbed her. Then she realized that the sparrows in the garden bushes below her window were making an unaccountable racket. A cat must have gotten in among them. She pulled the quilt over her head in an attempt to go back to sleep. But when she heard other noises from the stable yard, she pulled a shawl over her shoulders and went to her window. When she opened the sash, she saw nothing amiss. It was unusually mild for the eighth of February.

But later that morning the placid Old Biggin was almost uncontrollable as she drove to the Foundry. And her students were no better. If the sky hadn't been such a clear blue, she would have been certain a storm was about to strike. She had never been more relieved to see the hands of her watch approach twelve. "Your behavior has been most unacceptable this morning. Tomorrow you must be prepared to work harder, or I shall be obliged to have Mr. Told in." The rascals looked duly smitten at her words, but still they failed to leave the room in proper order.

Suddenly a great rumbling thunder shook the building and drowned out the noise of the departing children. Catherine turned to place an armful of books on her desk. But the desk was gone. As if the earth had suddenly spun off its axis, all the furniture in Catherine's room slid to the north wall.

The roaring and shaking continued for minutes that seemed like hours. As the earth heaved, the doors and windows in her room burst open. Bricks from the crumbling chimney fell past her window.

Leaning against the undulating wall for support, Catherine felt a kind of terror she had never known. As her knees gave way and she slid to the floor, she relived her childhood experience of falling off a horse, but now not even the earth was solid. All the fears she thought conquered swamped her again. Where was Philip?

When at last the rolling earth subsided, Catherine didn't move. She suddenly realized how much she had come to rely on Philip in the past months. He was the person she could always turn to, even when the foundations of the earth shook. She had sensed this, but she had never experienced so deeply her need of his calm stability.

And then as if in answer to the cry of her heart, Philip rushed into the room. "Catherine, are you all right? I was so afraid I wouldn't find you—that you might be hurt or . . ." He made a muffled choking sound.

She blinked in unbelief at his sudden appearance. She had not even known he was at the Foundary that day. Now here was a solid core of stability in a world with no underpinnings. "I—I'm . . ." She wanted to say she was fine, but found she was so shaken she couldn't speak. And her stomach was rolling so she was afraid she might be sick. All she could do was hold her hand out to him.

When his hand closed over hers, warm and strong, enough of her tension eased to allow the tears to spill from her eyes. Her whole body began to tremble. Philip slipped to the floor beside her and held her in his arms while she shook as hard as if the earthquake were repeating itself.

At last she relaxed enough to be able to rest her head on his shoulder. The comfort was indescribable. She could have continued so for hours, but the sound of running feet and excited voices in the courtyard intruded.

"We must help." Philip got to his feet and extended a hand to Catherine.

"Do you think there's much damage?" She surveyed the chaos of her room.

"There's sure to be a great deal in the poorer parts of town. Pray that there won't be a fire."

They had just moved into the courtyard when the second shock struck, this even harder than the first. Catherine was certain the earth would split apart beneath her feet. But Philip held her. And even in the midst of the terrified shrieks, the crash of falling bricks, and the roar of the jolting earth, Catherine knew she could not live without this man's support. Even if it meant going to the ends of the earth—even to America. Life without Philip was unthinkable.

That decision filled Catherine with peace. In the midst of the turmoil around her, her heart was calm. And she knew she had made the right decision. "My peace I give unto you: not as the world giveth . . ." Peace was the one emotion Satan could not counterfeit. It was the complete assurance of being in God's will.

And Catherine sorely needed that peace in the days to come because internal peace was the only quiet available. A throng of frightened people crowded into the damaged Foundery in last-minute hope of turning aside the wrath of God by repenting. Affluent, smug London had needed this reminder of the wrath of God and the judgment to come, and Ned had been unwittingly prophetic in saying that squabbling Society members needed shaking up. Now a frenzied earthquake theology spelled the end of optimism. Londoners' nerves became raw, incited by such predictions as Sir Isaac Newton's: "Jupiter is going to approach so close to the earth as possibly to brush it."

Whitefield and Wesley conducted all-night services for those too wrought-up to sleep and those who no longer had a bed to go home to. Philip held open-air services in Hyde Park. As on their circuit ride, Catherine frequently accompanied him and led the singing. The favorite song was Isaac Watts's: "O God, our help in ages past, / Our hope for years to come, / Our shelter from the stormy blast, / And our eternal Home!"

The crowd sang with a lustiness brought on by desperation, and then listened to the preacher as drowning men cling to a lifeline. Philip chose Isaiah 2 as his theme: "The haughtiness of men shall be made low; and the Lord alone shall be exalted in that day . . . for the glory of his majesty, when he ariseth to shake terribly the earth."

At the mention of shaking earth, cries of fear rose from the women and shouts of "amen" and "'s truth" from the men. Then Philip read to them the reassuring words from Psalm 46—that God was their refuge and strength, their help in trouble. They need not fear, though the earth be removed and the mountains fall into the sea. The preacher went on to explain the way to find refuge in such a God.

Catherine saw what a pillar of strength Philip was, as he led these frightened people to an understanding of the comfort and security God had for them. And she renewed her vow to stay by his side—that is, if he should want her to do so.

A few days later, when Catherine and Philip went to Chitty Lane to call on Elmira Smithson, they were appalled at the desolation the earthquake had wrought in the slum areas of the city. Although an ancient building code required the use of brick in order to prevent fire, no one could afford to pay any attention to the code, and the flimsy lath and plaster buildings had crumbled like sand castles.

Elmira was attempting to shelter her family in a room that now had only three walls. "You must come with us," Catherine said, as she picked up little Susanna and started toward the carriage.

"But where'll we go?" Elmira cried, her voice showing how torn she was between hope and despair.

Catherine stopped. She could think of nothing. She couldn't take them home with her. Durial would never hear of it. The spare rooms at the Foundery were already bursting with now-homeless Society members. There was not an extra inch in Philip's room.

Then Catherine thought of a place where there was space aplenty. "To Park Lane," she said.

The Countess of Huntingdon's butler did not so much as raise an eyebrow at the sight of the dirty, ill-clothed persons with Miss Perronet and Mr. Ferrar. "Please come in. I will see if Her Ladyship is at home."

Her Ladyship was. "This is most convenient." She bustled into the reception hall wearing a black cloak and a dark straw bonnet over her lace cap. "Lady Fanny and I were just setting out to deliver baskets of food to the needy. It is much better that they should come to me. Rettkin!" The butler materialized out of nowhere. "See that these children are fed and properly clothed. Their mother shall accompany me and direct my charities to the most deserving. I do abhor the thought of bestowing gifts upon the undeserving. You shall be a great help to me in my work, Mrs.—ah, I don't believe we've been introduced."

Her head spinning as always from encounters with the countess, Catherine accompanied an open-mouthed Isaiah and his brother and sisters to the housemaid's quarters and saw that they were settled before she left. "And now you shall have no excuse for coming to school with dirty hands, Isaiah," she said with a smile.

The winter evening was closing in fast when Catherine and Philip left Park Lane. "I must return you to your brother," Philip said. "The quake has turned many Londoners' minds to the judgment of God; but an equal number have adopted the philosophy of 'eat, drink, and be merry, for tomorrow ye die.' The streets are not safe for a woman."

Catherine sighed. "I expect you are right. But I had hoped we might call on Mr. Smithson and inform him of his family's good fortune."

"Tomorrow," Philip promised.

Catherine had had no time alone with Philip since the cataclysm. She could not speak to him of her new resolve unless he gave her an opening, some encouragement, just the slightest chink in the wall he kept around himself. But Philip's wall of isolation was perhaps the only one in London not cracked by the earthquake.

The next day Catherine saw that the walls of the Fleet were likewise intact. Outside, the mob listened to a thundering street preacher: "Earthquakes, by their majesty and dreadful horror, show God's hand stretched out in anger. This is why they are specially frightful. They are sudden, unavoidable, and threaten us with a peculiarly dreadful form of death."

A high shriek rose above the wailing of the crowd, and several women sank to the ground.

"The preservation of London was a miracle. God deliberately refrained from destroying the city, but damnation will have its numbers, come when it will . . ."

As the lamentation of the mob rose to a higher pitch, Catherine was for once grateful for the doors of the Fleet which cut her off from the sound.

To her relief, Smithson was sober today and eager for news. "I've 'eard tell such tales about London—tell me what it's like."

Catherine told him what had happened to Elmira and his children, holding her breath after mentioning the Countess of Huntingdon. She remembered Smithson's earlier resistance to "evangelical toffs mucking about in his affairs." But today his gratitude was wholehearted.

He even allowed Philip to read the Bible to him and the others in his cell. Philip chose Acts 16, explaining, "This is the story of others unfairly imprisoned at the time of an earthquake." He read of Paul and Silas being beaten and cast into prison where they prayed and sang praise to God. When he reached the part about the earthquake that shook the foundations of the prison and broke the prisoners' chains, the inmates gasped in amazement.

"Lor', I wisht the quake 'ad broken the Fleet down," a prisoner said.

"That's th' only way you'll see th' light o' day, Uriah."

Philip went on reading above the comments. The convicts erupted in jeers when Paul and Silas chose to remain in jail rather than escape, but Dick Smithson was silent. Indeed, he was so deep in thought when his visitors left that he did not even bid them farewell.

When Catherine arrived home, she walked into another crisis. Durial had been listening to a preacher at the Greenwich Village green that afternoon. Her high-strung nerves were now at the breaking point. She demanded the family leave London, and nothing Ned could say had any effect in calming her.

"Allow that I know what the preacher said, Husband. And allow me to judge the good sense his words made. Listen to his reasoning. This present earth, a very unsatisfactory second version of the first earth more or less destroyed by the flood, is going to end in a great conflagration that will burn it up. The fire will naturally begin at Rome, the headquarters of the Antichrist, but England is sure to be a particularly unpleasant spot because of our extensive coalfields."

"Durial!" Ned was never a patient man, and his wife's vapors drove him to distraction. "If the entire earth and especially all of England is to be burned up, what can it matter *where* we are living when it happens? My work is here."

"But you can take work elsewhere." Durial's voice rose another pitch. "I do not wish to compare London to Sodom, for London contains many good people, but because of its size it also contains a proportionately large number of evil people. And setting aside all other considerations, London, by reason of its crowded and insecure buildings, is of all places the most dangerous."

Ned turned away.

Durial flung herself across the room at him. "Do not turn your back on me. If our baby had lived, if I could have given you a child, you would not treat me so!" Racking sobs began to shake her body.

Ned turned and took his wife in his arms. "Durial, Durial. I will write to my father. Perhaps he will know of something."

Catherine, who had not intended to eavesdrop, fled to her room. It had been a full month since the earthquake; surely the hysteria would soon die down. People would rebuild their chimneys, replace their crockery, and reglaze their windows, and the great London earthquake would become nothing more than a memory.

Catherine gratefully accepted Audrey's offer to brush her hair for her. "Mmm, that feels good, Audrey. Thank you. Please snuff my candles on the way out. I feel as if I could sleep till the day of doom."

Those words were the first thing Catherine thought of early the next morning when an eruption of the earth broke forth with a thunderous roar and tumultuous shaking. Catherine jumped up with a cry, thinking the powder house on the green had exploded. But as her writing desk lurched, chairs shook, doors slammed, windows rattled, pewter and crockery clattered from their shelves, and the great elm tree outside her window crashed to the earth, sending shards of broken glass flying across her room, Catherine knew London was being visited by yet another earthquake.

13

$\mathcal{A}$ sharp cry, followed by a moaning wail, tore through the house. At first Catherine thought Durial was hurt. Then she realized the cry had come from the servants' quarters. She shook the bits of broken glass out of her slippers and off her shawl before donning them and running in the direction of the noise. When she arrived, along with the rest of the household, at Audrey's room, she found the maid sitting in a tangle of bedclothes, smashed crockery, and disordered furniture, cradling an oddly twisted arm and shrieking, "It threw me outta bed, it did. Just threw me out. My arm 'it the trunk, owww!"

"All right, Audrey, you will stop shrieking so that we can see to your injuries." Durial waded through the shambles. Her housekeeping instincts aroused by the disarray, she began giving orders for the care of Audrey and the righting of the room. Catherine smiled. All her sister-in-law needed to take her mind off her troubles was a house to clean. By the end of the day the house would not only be orderly, but also freshly scrubbed, and all the broken dishes replaced and on the shelf.

But not everywhere in London was the damage so quickly repaired. This quake was far more violent than the first, and buildings damaged by the first were leveled by the second.

People frightened by the first were terrified now. All over the city, church bells rang of their own accord, adding to the noise and confusion. People had run into the streets in their nightclothes and were still milling about hours later when Catherine arrived at the Foundery. The panic continued for days. In spite of the attempts of Wesley and other clergymen to calm their fears, the people flocked to the prophets of doom who shouted at the tops of their voices on every street corner, "The end of the world is at hand. Prepare to meet thy Maker."

In order to be of more help in the emergency, Catherine moved into London temporarily, staying with her sister, Elizabeth Briggs, in her newly established home. A small room that Elizabeth usually used for a private sitting room was at Catherine's disposal whenever she could snatch a few hours of sleep.

After a week of such a schedule, John Wesley fell ill, putting an even greater burden on Society members. In spite of the fact that they were working almost twenty-four hours a day in the same building, Catherine seldom saw Philip. But when she did, his calm self-containment and quiet efficiency reaffirmed her confidence that he was the one God had prepared for her.

After Catherine had spent a particularly tiring day of dispensing soup and changing dirty bandages for the charity school children, Philip came to her. She gave him a bowl of soup and bandaged a scrape on his hand, as if he were one of her charges.

When he had finished eating, she said, "I have heard rumors of damage and riots in the Fleet. Perhaps we should visit Dick Smithson?"

"I would not take you into that danger. There is no knowing what the rabble may be up to."

"Nonsense!" A flicker of a smile crossed Catherine's face; here was her chance to tell Philip a little of what she felt. "I am more than willing to go anywhere you go, to face anything you face." She said the words with confidence, ignoring the disquiet they caused in her heart.

He looked at her, a questioning wrinkle across his brow. "Catherine?"

The two of them were a small island of quiet in the tumult of post-earthquake London. She would have liked to remind him of the mad bulls, swollen rivers, and lighted fireworks she had already faced with him. She would have liked to tell him she was now willing to face an ocean voyage, wilderness living, and Indians with him. But she felt she had said quite enough, so she held out her arm. "Shall we go?"

The fact that the second shock had followed exactly four weeks to the day after the first gave rise to alarm in many quarters over what might follow on April 8.

The same preacher they had heard before still held forth from the corner near the Fleet. "What is God going to do next? Will He order winds to tear up our houses from their foundations and bury us in the ruins? Will He remove the raging distemper from the cattle and send the plague upon ourselves? Or—the Lord in His infinite mercy save us—He may command the earth to open her mouth and, the next time He ariseth to shake terribly the earth, command her to swallow us up alive, with our houses, our wives, our children, with all that appertains upon us."

A great weeping and moaning accompanied his words, much stronger in intensity than the first time Catherine heard him.

At first, the prison provost informed Philip that no amount of garnishment could buy his way in to visit a prisoner in the Fleet. But when Philip mentioned the name of the man they wished to visit, the response changed. "Oh, 'im. Guess that's all right then. Inside with yer." He pocketed the coins Philip offered.

Inside, a surprise met them. The jail seemed lighter, the air fresher, as if someone had opened all the windows. And then Catherine saw that was precisely what had happened. The dirty panes of glass from the small, barred windows had broken out, allowing fresh air and light into the prison. But more than that, at the end of the hall one section of the wall had broken away, forming a v-shaped passage to the street. The breech in the wall was well guarded, as a prisoner would need only to scramble up a small pile of fallen brick and leap through the hole to escape.

"Smithson!" the turnkey shouted.

To Catherine's surprise, one of the guards came forward. "Dick! You've been made a guard? What has happened?"

"It was like in that story you read us from the Bible," he addressed Philip. "Where the earthquake set the prisoners free. I gave a good piece o' thought to that and decided they was right to stay. Just 'a cause they was put there unfairly, didn't mean everybody was, and ya can't have murderers runnin' about the streets—wouldn't be safe for the women an' children. So when the quake shook that there 'ole in the wall, I stood in the gap, as ye might say."

"You prevented a jailbreak?" Catherine asked.

Dick's smile was sheepish behind his shaggy beard. "'Ad a might 'a trouble convincin' some it were a good idee. So I threw a few bricks 'ere and there to persuade 'em."

"And you've been promoted as a reward! Dick, that's wonderful! Will you get paid?"

He nodded. "Yep. Soon's my debt's paid off, I can go 'ome to Elmirey at night."

Catherine's heart sank. It would take more than a year for him to earn enough to pay his debt—unless he demanded bribes from the other prisoners. "Dick, that's wonderful, but you don't want to become like them." She pointed to the hardened jailers standing by the wall.

"No, I'd rather be more like 'im." He nodded toward Philip. "Thought I might try a piece o' prayin' or 'ymn singin'—course, I can't read the Bible none. Do you ever have any of these Methody Societies of yours in jails?"

Through the break in the wall, they could hear the street preacher still ranting, but Catherine could not feel alarmed by his words. She had just witnessed a miracle, and no fear for the future could diminish that glory. If only she and Philip could speak of the future—their future. Surely now, with London crumbled around them, they needed each other more than ever. She knew she needed Philip; if only he would say he needed her.

As they settled into the relative quiet of the carriage to drive back to the Foundery where Catherine would spend another night with Elizabeth, she thought, *Perhaps now he will speak. We are alone—perhaps now . . .*

And perhaps he did. But Catherine, worn out by the long days of work and emotion with only brief snatches of sleep, fell asleep to the swaying motion of the vehicle. And much to her surprise, she awoke late the next morning, not in the tiny closet off her sister's room where she had been staying, but in her room in Greenwich.

"How did I get here?" she asked Audrey, who was carrying on with her duties with one arm tied in a sling. Catherine recalled that just a year ago, Ned had been the one with a damaged arm. It seemed as if her life was ever to be punctuated with upheavals no matter how much she prayed for a more gentle calling.

"Mr. Ned brought you in sound asleep last night. The mistress sent him for you—said it wasn't right for you to be working day and night in London when you needed to be here making your earthquake gown."

"My what?" Catherine sat upright in her bed.

Audrey handed her a cup of coffee. "All the ladies is makin' 'em. Mistress 'as us all at it—but I'm not much good sewing with only one 'and."

"Audrey, what are you talking about?"

"Earthquake gowns. To wear for the all-night vigil when the final quake comes. Mistress says we'll all go out in the fields—since she can't convince Mr. Ned to take us clean out of London as some are doin'."

"That will be enough, Audrey. Thank you."

Catherine finished her coffee, dressed quickly, and hurried downstairs. Sure enough, Durial had assembled all the female servants in the south sitting room where each one was stitching intently on a garment of ivory muslin. While they stitched, Durial read to them from a printed earthquake sermon. She looked up as Catherine entered. "Hello, Sister. As you see, the next visitation of the Lord's hand shall not find us sleeping. I have ordered a length of muslin for you too."

The sound of an approaching horse eliminated the need for Catherine to reply. "Don't put down your sewing, any of you. I shall see to the door." She fled from the room, wondering what in the world she would do with such a garment. As if it would matter what one wore when being swallowed alive by the earth.

Her heart soared when she saw their visitor. She ran down the steps, and, as in all her dreams, Philip opened his arms and she went into them. For a moment they stood there in the morning sunshine, secure and belonging.

"I have come to speak to you," he said at last.

"Come into the front parlor. Everyone else is in back. You can't imagine what Durial has them doing."

"Making earthquake gowns?"

"How did you know?"

"It's all the rage in London. I called on the countess this morning, and even her household is set about it."

"Has the panic not subsided at all yet?" She led him to a small sofa.

"The countess said seven hundred coaches have been counted passing Hyde Park Corner with whole parties moving into the country. It is said lodging is unattainable in Windsor and nearby villages."

Catherine had no desire to continue a discussion of the earthquake now that she finally had Philip alone in a quiet room. She looked down at her hands, but she couldn't quite suppress the smile on her lips.

Still he hesitated, so she made an opening for him. "You

have determined to accept Mr. Whitefield's offer?" Why did those simple words make her think of walking into a dark night?

He gave her a deep, level look, but before he could reply, a carriage sounded on the drive. No servants appeared from the sewing circle, so Catherine went to the door. The sight of the beloved figure in a full-bottomed wig brought a joyous cry from her. "Father!" For the second time that morning, she flew into a caller's arms. "What a wonderful surprise! What brings you to London when everyone else is fleeing the city?"

"That is precisely what brought me, Child. Your mother could not rest until I could bring her my personal assurances that all her children in London are well. We have received the most alarming reports—"

A small figure bounded out of the carriage and threw herself into Catherine's arms as well. "Philothea!"

"Isn't it famous! I convinced Mother that Father shouldn't travel so far alone, and she could spare me much more easily than any of the boys." Then she saw Philip who had come into the hall to greet the arrivals, and she abandoned her sister for her idol. "I brought you a poppy-seed cake. We'll pretend it's your birthday."

Catherine ushered them all into the parlor and had turned to summon Durial when she saw that yet another coach had arrived. Perfect in its shiny fittings, with golden coronets on its doors, this coach carried the Countess of Huntingdon.

George Whitefield alighted first and offered his hand to assist Lady Huntingdon; then, as yet another surprise, Charles Wesley emerged behind her. The countess issued an order to her driver and then led the way into the house, past Catherine standing at the door.

"I have come to speak with you," she addressed Philip. "I do not know what is to be done with that man Smithson. Oh, hello, Vincent. What brings you to London? This is an insane time to be visiting the city—they say it will be level in a short time. But never mind. You're looking well." Without giving Vincent a chance to reply, she went on from her position in the center of the room.

"I paid Mr. Smithson's debts as you suggested, Philip, but he has declined my offer of a place on my estate at Donnington Park. What do you say to that?"

Whitefield answered for Philip, "My Lady, if he feels a calling to minister to those unfortunates in prison, are we to interfere with that?"

"Calling? What does one of his class know of a calling?"

"The disciples were simple men, My Lady. Our Lord called them," Whitefield said.

The countess tossed her head in the air with a sniff. Just then Ned and Durial entered, and the conversation became general. Not even the Countess of Huntingdon was able to upstage a reunion of the Perronet family.

Across the room Catherine sought to catch Philip's eye. He stood tall and alone in the corner, isolated from all the joyful family greetings. Catherine felt an overwhelming desire to reach him, to tell him she would be his family, that he never need be alone again. But Charles Wesley was beside her, and she must speak to him. "What has brought you to London?"

"I received word my brother was gravely ill—at death's door. I came to nurse him, but when I arrived, I found him in the quite capable hands of Mrs. Vazielle."

"Humph," the countess said. "Clutches is more like. It will not do, Charles. She must not ensnare him."

Charles nodded. "Indeed, I believe she is a woman of sorrowful spirit."

"She will not do." The countess issued her edict with another toss of her head and moved on around the room, instinctively playing hostess as if she were in her own London drawing room.

"And how is Sally? I haven't heard from her for months," Catherine asked.

Charles's face became somber. "My dearest is not well. The

babe miscarried. It may have been the shock of the first earth-quake . . ."

"Charles, I'm so sorry. Is there fear for her health?"

"No, no. The doctor says we may look forward to a full quiver. But this one is mourned."

And Catherine too ached for Sally's empty mother-arms, for the unheard baby laughter, for dreams unfulfilled—an ache of might-have-beens.

Again the question arose in her heart as she looked at Philip and wondered if her own dreams must also die before they could be born. *My God, where are You? You have promised a perfect way—but where? And when?*

Just then Vincent Perronet joined her and Charles. "Ah, Mr. Wesley, tell me of the work in your part of the country. Is there still a movement for separation?"

Catherine knew how strongly Charles opposed such ideas and listened carefully for his answer. "It seems the great shaking-up God gave us has not been without its consequence in the minds of the brethren. We had a conference of the northern and midlands Societies just a week ago. All agreed not to separate. So the wound is healed—slightly."

Catherine realized she had been holding her breath await-ing Charles's answer. Now it escaped in a great sigh. It seemed that suddenly in the very wake of destruction God was answer-ing her prayers. Was this His perfect time? The time she had so long awaited?

It seemed even more likely as Ned joined them and his father turned to him. "My Son, I have come not only as an emis-sary from your mother, but also as a petitioner in my own behalf."

"Sir?"

"I think you know from visiting my estate in Canterbury last year that Adisham has been looking for retirement. I can put him off no longer. He must be pensioned into a cottage and the burden of running the farm passed to younger, stronger hands. Would you consider being those hands, Ned?"

"Move to Canterbury? I must give it some thought. I believe Durial would like it above all things."

"And you, Ned? It should give you more uninterrupted time for hymn-writing, and the Societies in Kent are in need of a firm hand among them."

Catherine's head was reeling. This would solve Ned and Durial's problem. But what about hers? She looked across the room at the still-silent Philip. In the midst of the noisy room he was calm and detached. And yet he looked sad, as if instinctively missing the belonging he had never known.

She started toward him, but Philothea intervened. "Catherine, I'm longing to hear all about your earthquake adventures! Was it alarming? All we got in Shoreham was a gentle rolling—no more than a rocking chair."

And then Whitefield approached Philip, and Catherine heard him ask, "And what of my invitation? Have you decided to go to America with me?"

But Philip's voice was softer than Whitefield's, and she could not hear the answer.

14

*D*urial was at the height of her glory directing her well-trained servants and seeing to her guests' comfort. When Ned spoke briefly to her of Vincent's offer, she immediately declared that the entire company should stay to dinner in celebration. Her larders were up to any challenge—even to serving the Countess of Huntingdon on short notice. She dispatched Joseph from the stables to London to fetch Elizabeth and William Briggs so that all available family members might be there.

Ned and his father went into the study for further discussion of their plans, and Philothea requested Catherine to show her around the house and garden. As she left the parlor, Catherine heard Whitefield and Philip discussing the plans for sailing to America, but only one voice was distinct. "America? Nonsense!" And the countess snapped her fan to punctuate her words.

After giving Philothea a quick tour, Catherine took her sister to the guest room to wash and change for dinner and retired to her own room to do the same. Audrey brought her a brass can of hot water from the kitchen, and Catherine reveled in repeatedly splashing her face and arms as if she could wash away the fatigue and strain of the past weeks.

But when she turned to her mirror to arrange her curls, she was shocked at how clearly her recent fatigue and worry were written there. What was wrong? God had answered all her prayers—all but one. And surely it was only a matter of time—probably tomorrow Philip would call and their conversation would be uninterrupted. She had known for weeks what her answer would be. Then she stopped.

Suddenly she knew the cause of the weight around her heart and the hollow feeling in the center of her stomach. She had known peace the moment she acknowledged her love for Philip. But she had known nothing but internal turmoil, far greater than any caused by the earthquakes, over her decision to go to America. What of her criterion that if a step were directed of God, it would be accompanied by His peace?

Could the fact that she had been thwarted at every attempt to speak to Philip of her decision to go and the lack of peace over the decision mean she *wasn't* to go? It was true that she felt no real call to the work in America—no intense desire to minister in that field. But wasn't a desire to be with the minister himself enough? Had she mistaken her wish to be with Philip for a call to be a missionary? Must she choose between Philip and God's call? If that were the case, there could be no choice.

The arrival of yet another carriage told her the Briggses had arrived. She must go down and take her place in the family circle. Inside, Catherine felt nothing but a gaping hole where her dreams had been, but outside she wore her usual air of calm serenity. Durial's excellent meal choked her, and when she attempted to reply to a remark directed to her, her tight, controlled voice sounded more awful to her ears than if she had shouted.

Across the table Philip responded to a question from Charles Wesley in his slow, thoughtful voice and then looked across the table at her. For an awful moment their eyes held. Then he gave that tiny half-smile of his, and she could sit there no longer.

Summoning all her natural dignity, Catherine asked her hostess to excuse her and walked slowly to her room. Mechanically she went through all the motions of her night-time ritual and then drew the heavy side curtains of her bed around her. She had no sense of God's presence with her in that small enclosure. She could only cling to her determination to believe that He was still there.

The next morning it seemed a miracle to her that she had slept, that the sun had risen again, that birds were singing. Such things were entirely alien to the desolation inside her. Durial was surprised by her announcement that she did not intend to go in to the Foundery that day.

"Regular lessons have not been resumed yet; I am certain they can get along very well without me."

"A very wise decision, Catherine. I am just surprised you would take so sensible a course. After all, your earthquake gown is yet unfinished. And now we must make one for Philothea too, as Father Perronet does not intend to return to Shoreham before the end of the week. And all the china must be packed. How fortunate that one packing will suffice for earthquake protection and for our removal to Canterbury. I can think of no more satisfactory solution for our needs. Will you live with Elizabeth when we are gone? That seems far the best plan—assuming there remains a London to be lived in, that is."

Durial thrust Catherine's half-sewn gown into her hands and began cutting her final length of muslin for Philothea. "How fortunate that I have just enough fabric left. Now we must decide whether to hold our vigil in the meadows by Hither Green or take to a boat in the Thames. Which do you think would be the best, Ned?"

Edward looked up from the manuscript of a poem he was composing. "Where do you think we'd find a boat? Besides, those gowns will show off to the best advantage in an open field."

Durial was completely unscathed by his sarcasm. "Yes, I suppose that is best. There's always the danger of a great wave swamping a boat. But I did think that in case of fire, the river might be a wise choice."

"Well, to the best of my knowledge, there are no coal fields under Hither Green Meadow, so you should be quite safe there from a conflagration."

The prophets had pinpointed the night of April 4 or early morning of April 5, so all day Wednesday Durial worked everyone around her to a frenzy, storing the last of the crockery and silver, securing the furniture with ropes, and packing huge hampers of food. "If the destruction is great, we may have to live in the open for some time. Audrey, you and Joseph fill the pony cart with blankets."

Catherine obeyed, as did all the others, including Vincent Perronet. Hysteria was in the air, and there was no sense in trying to fight it. "Ned," Vincent admonished his son about to depart for the Foundery, "could you bring an extra hymnal or two from the book room? We might keep the folks occupied with a candlelight hymn-sing."

Ned agreed and assured Durial for the seventh time that he would not return late from his visit to encourage John Wesley in his convalescence.

By the time Ned returned at five o'clock, Durial had household and carriages in perfect order and all the females of the family and staff properly clad in their earthquake gowns. "Yes, I suppose you must take your cloaks, but it does seem a pity to cover the gowns. Although I imagine by the time it's really cold it will be dark also. But then if great fires start, you won't need a wrap, will you?"

Catherine was pleased with Ned's news that the countess would join them at the meadow. She was bringing her household staff and the Smithson family as something of a celebration for the newly reunited family. But then she was alarmed at his next piece of information. "George Whitefield left yesterday for his parents' home in Gloucester, so she is bringing Philip in place of her private chaplain."

Catherine climbed into the carriage next to Philothea and was thankful for her sister's chatter all the way to the meadow. The exit route from London was choked with carriages, horseback riders, and pedestrians. A festival air accompanied the evacuees as they called and waved to their friends. But Catherine sat motionless. Philip would be there tonight. She was certain he would speak to her, and she would much rather encounter an earthquake than to tell him she couldn't go to America with him.

The sun was setting when they reached Hither Green. Durial selected a pleasant spot near a spinney of trees and directed the servants to spread out rugs on the grass. Catherine remained inside the carriage as long as possible; but when the countess's party arrived and chose to park not far from them, she could no longer remain hidden. "Come, Cath! Let's go listen to the preachers!" Philothea tugged at her hand.

They walked across the meadow grass, their gowns devoid of familiar hoops and panniers and swishing around their ankles. They stood behind a crowd listening to a doomsaying preacher. "It says it right here in the Book of Matthew, 'There shall be earthquakes in divers places. All these are the beginning of sorrows.'" A moan went up from the overwrought audience. "'Then shall they deliver you up to be afflicted, and shall kill you . . .'"

A warm hand touched Catherine's shoulder, and Philip's deep voice said, "He seems to be overlooking the exhortation to avoid the false prophets that come at that time."

It was now dark, and as Catherine turned, the glow of the lantern Philip carried fell on his hair and gentle eyes. She had never guessed that her determination to follow God could teeter so precariously.

"Durial sent me to fetch you. She is serving supper from the hampers."

Philothea hung on Philip's arm and fairly skipped across the meadow with him, leaving Catherine to walk quietly beside them, wearing the natural calm solemnity of her expression that showed nothing of the pain she was feeling. Was this what it meant to love—truly to love? This caring so much you thought you couldn't stand it? And then not being able to do anything about it?

She sat on the rug Durial indicated. She held her plate of food and slipped enough of it to Isaiah Smithson to make it appear she had eaten and then sent her greetings to his parents who were eating with the servants. And she listened to the countess holding forth: "England is darkened with clouds of ignorance and sin. If God spares us this night, I shall turn upon our country the light of divine truth. The church is slumbering at ease, benumbed by the poisonous influence of error. I shall arouse the careless sleepers and apply the gospel antidote. Throughout England, Wales, Scotland, and Ireland I shall repair the ancient altars and enkindle fresh fires. If we are spared the fires of judgment tonight . . ." But when Ned and her father began gathering the party together to sing hymns, it was more than Catherine could bear. She slipped away to sit in the carriage.

Across the meadow candles and lanterns flickered like overgrown fireflies, and the voices of the singers carried to her on the night air: "All hail the power of Jesus' name! / Let angels prostrate fall . . ."

They had begun the third song when Catherine heard a soft rap at the carriage door. At first it was so gentle she thought she was mistaken, but then she saw Philip's dear craggy profile in the moonlight.

"Catherine, may I come in? I must speak to you." The calmness of his voice sounded as forced as was her effort at sounding cheerful as she offered him the seat facing her.

It seemed he dreaded what he would say as much as Catherine dreaded the reply she must give. He regarded her in silence, a soft glow of moonlight falling through the carriage window. For a moment she who had learned to read him so well saw an opening, a readiness to speak, and then something snapped shut inside.

Now that they were together, they must speak. If only she could reach him, pry open that spring that always closed her out. Philip seemed to realize how near he had come to letting the barrier down. He put his hands over his face as if to rebuild the piece he'd let fall from the wall.

At last he took a breath so deep that Catherine felt as if the whole carriage shook. "I shouldn't have come. I don't know why I did. Catherine, I cannot speak. I long to, but I may not. Surely you know how I feel about you, how tenderly I regard you. I had hoped to have something to offer you. But I have nothing."

And the barrier was sealed again.

In the dimness of the night, from the dark of her own pain, Catherine reached out to him and took his hand. "Nothing to offer but your dear self, Philip."

The term of endearment seem to wound him. He pulled his hand away. "I had hoped to have something of substance—a place to offer you."

"And I had hoped to accept—"

"Catherine, I have refused Mr. Whitefield's offer. Now I have nothing. I tried to accept, but it was wrong. I was considering it for the wrong reasons—to make a home to offer you, not to serve God."

The relief was overwhelming. For long minutes Catherine could only swallow. At last the burning lump in her throat dissolved, and she could pray, *Thank You, my God, thank You.*

"Catherine, I cannot tell you."

With a sudden force that would make an observer think the earthquake had struck the Perronet carriage, Catherine moved across the seat and into Philip's arms. "Oh, Philip, that's the best news I've ever heard. Why didn't you tell me? I had come to the same conclusion. I was determined to go in order to be with you, but then I knew it was wrong. I thought you were going to ask me to go, and I should have to refuse you. Oh, Philip!"

And at last, after months of waiting, he kissed her—or she kissed him. It was impossible to tell. But as the choir in the meadow sang, "Love divine, all loves excelling, / Joy of heav'n to earth come down," the two in the carriage knew a bit of that divine love on earth.

Then Philip pulled away. "It's not possible. Life's not really that good—not mine."

"I intend to do my best to see that it is from here on."

"Catherine, in my whole life I've never loved anyone—nor anyone me. I'm afraid l don't know how to go about this."

She traced the hollow of his cheek with a gentle finger. "You're doing very well for a beginner."

But the tender mood broke as he firmly set her back on her own side of the carriage. "What was I thinking? Forgive me. Catherine, nothing has changed. The fact still remains that l am a foundling without place or prospect. Even if I were such a self-ish bounder as to ask you to sacrifice yourself to me, it must be clear to you that the honorable, respected, not to mention well-to-do Vincent Perronet would never give his daughter to one with such a background."

"Philip, what nonsense! My father believes we are all equal before God, all sons and heirs. There are no foundlings in God's family."

"Spiritually, I do not doubt that. But in the terms of this world I am a foundling who—"

"A foundling who has found grace in the sight of God and favor in the eyes of the woman who loves him."

This time he came to her across the carriage width, and at long last everything about him told her that he had come home. Philip had found a place of belonging as he had never belonged before.

Nothing was solved, but for the moment, having Philip love her and loving him in return was enough. And she had her firm faith that God would guide them, would open a door for them in time.

The singers in the meadow began another hymn. Catherine turned her head slightly from Philip's shoulder and looked out the small window. Across the meadow candles and lanterns flickered, and the women's pale muslin gowns ruffled in a gentle predawn breeze. The night appointed for terror and catastrophe was flooded with peace and beauty. She turned back to Philip and closed her eyes.

Perhaps they dozed, because streaks of red and gold were filling the eastern sky when a sharp rap on the carriage door brought its occupants back to the present world.

"Well, it appears the hand of the avenging angel has passed us by. But I must say, if I were the Almighty, I'd be hard pressed to find a reason to spare this lot." The Countess of Huntingdon held the door for them to step out. "I have ordered breakfast served, and I have an announcement for which you might wish to be present."

Everyone looked drowsy after the night's vigil but not the least bit chagrined that they had awaited a calamity that failed to occur. Joseph, Audrey, and Elmira Smithson were passing around cider and pork pie as the morning sun broke over the meadow. Standing in the center of the group, his arms held up to heaven, Vincent Perronet prayed, "For our deliverance, our Father, we thank Thee. Help the lives which Thou hast spared to be lived worthily unto Thee. Amen."

And the people who had sung through most of the night responded, "Glory be to the Father and to the Son, and to the Holy Ghost. As it was in the beginning, is now and ever shall be, world without end, amen."

Then Lady Huntingdon took center stage. "Since the world has not ended, it appears the Almighty intends that we should go on with our work. My chaplain, Mr. Whitefield, is soon to depart for America, and I shall be in need of a replacement for his services. Therefore, I appoint Mr. Philip Ferrar to fill his vacancy." She looked at Philip. "You, sir, are not to go to America. I have determined it will not suit."

Catherine gasped and turned to Philip. The look of astonishment on his face told her he had no idea this was coming.

"This position is, of course, only temporary." Her Ladyship paused. "I have determined to build a private chapel in Tunbridge Wells and install a permanent chaplain there. Mr. Ferrar, you shall have that position."

With the precision with which he did everything, Philip rose to his feet and bowed to the countess. "Yes, Your Ladyship."

Only Catherine saw the twinkle of amusement behind his smile of pleasure.

"And," the countess turned a half-circle to take in the entire company and then focused directly on Philip, "you are to marry this young lady."

The amusement and pleasure on Philip's face were eclipsed by the look of open love he turned on Catherine as he extended his hand to help her to her feet.

"Yes, Your Ladyship." They replied to the countess, but they looked only at each other.

All Hail the Power

EDWARD PERRONET
Alt. by John Rippon

OLIVER HOLDEN

1. All Hail the pow'r of Je-sus' name! Let an-gels pros-trate fall;
2. Ye cho-sen seed of Is-real's race, Ye ran-somed from the fall,
3. Let ev-'ry kin-dred, ev-'ry tribe, On this ter-res-trial ball,
4. O that with yon-der sa-cred throng We at His feet may fall!

Bring forth the roy-al di-a-dem, And crown Him Lord of all;
Hail Him who saves you by His grace And crown Him Lord of all;
To Him all maj-es-ty as-cribe, And crown Him Lord of all;
We'll join the ev-e-last-ing song, And crown Him Lord of all;

Bring forth the ro-yal di-a-dem And crown Him Lord of all;
Hail Him who saves you by His grace, And crown Him Lord of all;
To Him all maj-es-ty as-cribe, And crown Him Lord of all;
We'll join the ev-er-last-ing song, And crown Him Lord of all;

Historical Footnote

*T*his book is a work of fiction with a great deal of history woven in. Especially when many of the characters are familiar to the reader, it can be important to separate fact from fiction. The accounts given of the Wesleys, the Foundery, the Methodist Society, the Countess of Huntingdon, George Whitefield, and William Law are accurate, taken from the journals and biographies listed in the bibliography.

The earthquakes and reactions to them are matters of historical record; the "earthquake theology" sermons were preached as quoted.

The story of the Perronets is as accurate as I could make it, but here the novelist's imagination was called into greater service, as the references to members of this large family in journals and historical accounts are tantalizingly brief. I have used all I could learn of Catherine. She was indeed on the eligibility list John Wesley presented to Charles, but of her later life nothing is known.

Philip Ferrar is entirely fictional, but he is in many ways a composite of the early Methodist preachers recorded in history. Most of his sermons were patterned on John Wesley's. None of the hardships encountered on the preaching tours are made up. All are taken from the journals of John and Charles Wesley and George Whitefield. As Betty Waller, who previewed the manuscript dedicated to her, said, "And to think, we sit Sunday after Sunday in our nice comfortable pews and don't have any idea what others went through for our faith."

Emmanuel College has made posthumous amends to William Law for the deprivation of his Fellowship. Only two

Emmanuel men have been honored by being pictured in the stained glass windows of its chapel—John Harvard and William Law. On April 28, 1961, the rector and people of King's Cliffe held a service to commemorate the two-hundredth anniversary of Law's death. A party of members of Emmanuel, including the master, several fellows, and the whole of the chapel choir, went up to King's Cliffe for the occasion.

In spite of Wesley's great desire that the people saved under Methodist preaching would become the "saving salt" for the Church of England, that was not to happen. In 1784 Wesley sat in an Anglican service and heard a tirade against Methodists. That night he sorrowfully recorded in his *Journal*, "All who preach thus will drive the Methodists from the church, in spite of all that I can do." That is what happened after Wesley died in 1791. Not all ties with the establishment were broken, however; for when Wesley's New Chapel, built in 1778, was reopened after complete restoration on All Saint's Day in 1978, H.R.H. Queen Elizabeth II attended. Her comment as she thanked the minister at the door was, "You Methodists do sing loudly."

The church of St. Peter and St. Paul at Shoreham continues to serve its parish under the guidance of the present vicar, Geoffrey Sedgwick Simpson, an American from Vermont. I visited Shoreham on a day filled with sunshine, flowers, and birdsong and suggested to the vicar that he had chosen to serve in Shoreham because he didn't want to wait until the afterlife for Heaven.

I wish to express my deep appreciation to John Charles Pollock who read my manuscript for solecisms and anachronisms; and to Cyril Skinner, managing curator, and Douglas A. Wollen, historian, who were so helpful during my research at Wesley's New Chapel.

DONNA FLETCHER CROW

Time Line
THE CAMBRIDGE CHRONICLES

UNITED STATES		ENGLAND
George Whitefield begins preaching	1738	John Wesley's Aldersgate experience
French and Indian War	1756	
	1760	George III crowned
	1760	Lady Huntingdon opens chapel in Bath
	1766	Stamp Act passed
Boston Tea Party	1773	Rowland Hill ordained
The Revolutionary War	1776	The American War
	1787	Wilberforce begins antislavery campaign
Constitution ratified	1788	
George Washington elected President	1789	
	1799	Church Missionary Society founded
	1805	Lord Nelson wins Battle of Trafalgar
	1807	Parliament bans slave trade
War of 1812	1812	Charles Simeon begins Conversation Parties
	1815	Waterloo
Missouri Compromise	1820	George IV crowned
John Quincy Adams elected President	1825	
	1830	William IV crowned
Temperance Union founded	1833	William Wilberforce dies
Texas Independence	1836	Charles Simeon dies
	1837	Queen Victoria crowned
Susan B. Anthony Campaigns	1848	
California Gold Rush	1849	
	1851	Crystal Palace opens
Uncle Tom's Cabin published	1852	
	1854	Florence Nightingale goes to Crimean War
Abraham Lincoln elected President	1860	
Emancipation Proclamation	1863	
	1865	Hudson Taylor founds China Inland Mission
Transcontinental Railroad completed	1869	
	1877	D. L. Moody and Ira Sankey London revivals
Thomas Edison invents light bulb	1879	
	1885	Cambridge Seven join China Inland Mission

Word List

Abecedarian—an ABC book that also taught prayers and the rudiments of the Christian religion

Bagnio—brothel

Butter pond pudding—steamed pudding served in a pond of melted butter

Cassock—long, close garment worn by clergy

Chaise—a light carriage or pleasure vehicle

Chalybeate—spring water containing salts of iron

Collop—a small slice of meat, such as a rasher of bacon

Commination—a recital of God's anger and judgment against sinners

Curate—an assistant to an Anglican vicar

Dishabille—casual clothing

Farthing—smallest coin of English currency, valued at 1/4 penny

Fichu—a kerchief of fine white fabric draped over the shoulders and fastened in front to fill in a low neckline

Foundery—abandoned ironworks John Wesley bought in 1739 near Moorfields and converted into chapels, school, medical clinic, living quarters, etc., for the Methodist Society

Hectic fever—a fluctuating but persistent fever, such as accompanying tuberculosis

Jugged pigeons—pigeons stewed in an earthenware jug

Lappets—lace streamers falling from cap to shoulders

Lawn—a sheer, plain-woven cotton or linen fabric, as used in the sleeves of an Anglican bishop's robes

Methodist Society—a religious society open to all people, designed to enrich and purify all churches. Societies promoted preaching, fellowship meetings, Sunday schools, day schools, orphanages, and numerous other services for members' faith, education, health, and well-being

Nonconformist (dissenter)—member of a religious body separated from the Church of England

Nonjuror—Anglican clergyman who refused to take the oath of allegiance to William and Mary and their descendants

Oast house—a conical-shaped kiln used for drying hops or malt

Open gown—dress with skirt open in front below waist to reveal an ornate petticoat

Ordinary—a clergyman appointed to give spiritual counsel to condemned criminals; an official position comparable to chaplain

Pannier—hooped petticoat that supported a skirt

Pease porridge—split pea soup

Quid—slang for one pound sterling

Rector or vicar—clergyman of the Church of England who has charge of a parish

Riding pillion—to sit behind the saddle on a small pad

Round gown—dress with skirt closed in front, not showing petticoat

Shilling—British coin equivalent to U.S. nickel

Sizar—Cambridge student who receives college expenses in return for acting as servant to other students

St. Dunstan—religious reformer who served as Archbishop of Canterbury from 959 to 988

Syllabarium—a section of a primer that began with two-letter syllables and gradually increased in length until six-syllable words were taught

Tutball—an early form of cricket

Verger—an official in church who serves as caretaker and attendant

Bibliography

Babington, Anthony. *The English Bastille*. New York: St. Martin's Press, 1971.

Barker, Esther T. *Lady Huntingdon, Whitefield, and the Wesleys*. Private printing, 1984.

Boyle, P. *The Fashionable Court Guide, or Town Visiting Directory for the Year 1792*. London.

Brailsford, Mabel Richmond. *A Tale of Two Brothers, John and Charles Wesley*. New York: Oxford University Press, 1954.

Kendrick, T. D. *The London Earthquake*. London: Methuen & Co., Ltd., 1956.

Knight, Helen. *Lady Huntington [sic.] and Her Friends*. New York: American Tract Society, 1853.

"William Law: A Bicentenary" (including the text of Professor Chadwick's sermon preprinted from *The Anglican World*). *The Emmanuel College Magazine* 43 (1960-61).

Law, William. *A Serious Call to a Devout and Holy Life*. London: J. M. Dent & Sons Ltd., 1906.

"Law's Serious Call." *The Emmanuel College Magazine* 31 (1937-38).

McClure, Ruth. *Coram's Children, the London Foundling Hospital in the Eighteenth Century*. New Haven: Yale University Press, 1981.

Member of the Houses of Shirley and Hastings. *The Life and Times of Selina Countess of Huntingdon*. London: William Edward Painter, Strand, 1844.

Mitchell, T. Crichton. *The Wesley Century*. Vol. 2. Kansas City: Beacon Hill Press, 1984.

Moreton, G. *Memorials of the Birthplace and Residence of the Rev. Wm. Law M.S. at King's Cliffe in Northhamptonshire*. London: The London Printing Works, 1895.

Pollock, John. *George Whitefield and the Great Awakening*. New York: Doubleday & Co., 1972.

Lord Sheffield, John. *Miscellaneous Works of Edward Gibbon, Esq.* Vol. 1. London: 1796.

Smith, Nila Banton. *American Reading Instruction*. Newark: International Reading Association, 1974.

Tighe, Richard. *A Short Account of the Life and Writings of the Late Rev. William Law, A.M.* London: J. Hatchard, 1813.

Told, Silas. "An Account of Mr. Silas Told" (reprinted from *Life and Adventures of Silas Told*). *The Arminian Magazine* 11 (1788).

Tyerman, L. *The Life and Times of John Wesley.* Vol. 3. London: Hodder & Stoughton, 1880.

Wesley, Charles. *The Journal of Charles Wesley.* 1849 ed. Ed. Thomas Jackson. Grand Rapids: Baker Book House.

Wesley, John. *Journal.* Standard ed. 8 vols. Ed. Nehemiah Curnock. 1909-1916.